THE APPRENTICE'S MASTERPIECE

A STORY OF MEDIEVAL SPAIN

Melanie Little

annick press
toronto + new york + vancouver

Edited by Barbara Pulling
Copy edited by Heather Sangster
Proofread by Elizabeth McLean
Cover and interior design by Irvin Cheung / iCheung Design, inc.
Cover and interior illustrations by Shelagh Armstrong

We acknowledge the support of the Canada Council for the Arts, the Ontario Arts Council, and the Government of Canada through the Book Publishing Industry Development Program (BPIDP) for our publishing activities.

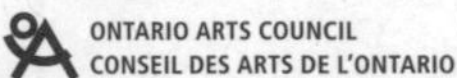

Cataloguing in Publication
Little, Melanie, date-
The apprentice's masterpiece : a story of medieval Spain / Melanie Little.
Novel written in verse.
ISBN 978-1-55451-117-4.— ISBN 978-1-55451-190-7
1. Inquisition— Spain —Juvenile fiction.
2. Jews— Spain —History—Expulsion, 1492—Juvenile fiction. I. Title.
PS8573.I857A66 2008 jC813'.6 C2007-905467-6

Published in the U.S.A. by
Annick Press (U.S.) Ltd.

Distributed in Canada by
Firefly Books Ltd.
66 Leek Crescent
Richmond Hill, ON
L4B 1H1

Distributed in the U.S.A. by
Firefly Books (U.S.) Inc.
P.O. Box 1338
Ellicott Station
Buffalo, NY 14205

Printed and bound in Canada

Preserving our environment

Annick Press chose Legacy TB Natural 100% post-consumer recycled paper for the pages of this book printed by Webcom Inc.

Mixed Sources
Product group from well-managed forests, controlled sources and recycled wood or fiber
www.fsc.org Cert no. SW-COC-002358
© 1996 Forest Stewardship Council

99%

Visit our website at **www.annickpress.com**

This book is dedicated to victims of intolerance everywhere, and to those who have resisted by asking questions, even if only of themselves.

You can burn the paper,
but you cannot burn what it contains;
I carry it within my heart.

Ibn Hazm, Cordoba
994 – 1064

Prologue

SPAIN HAS ALWAYS BEEN a place of stories. In fact, the first great novel, *Don Quixote*, came from Spain. Medieval Spaniards were enchanted by tales of knights and ladies, and even the kings and nobles loved the rather far-fetched story of their origin from the Greek demigod Hercules. But sometimes this fondness for storytelling had a dangerous side.

In the years leading up to what history books call the Golden Age of Spain, the country was divided into three separate kingdoms: Christian Castile in the center, Christian Aragon to the east, and the small but important Granada, ruled by the Muslim dynasty of the Nazrids, at the southern tip. On October 19, 1469, Prince Fernando, heir to the throne of Aragon, married Princess Isabella, heiress to the throne of Castile. The first stone on the road to the great dream of "One Spain" had been set.

But Spain had already had a Golden Age. From 711 A.D. until the twelfth century, it was known as the kingdom of al-Andalus, ruled by Muslims who had come from Damascus in Syria. The Muslims' holy book, the Koran, taught them to respect other religions—particularly those of the other "peoples of the book," Christians and Jews. The conquered Christians of al-Andalus were allowed to practice their own faith and speak their own language; so, too, were the Jews, who had been settled in Spain since Roman times. Yet many chose to learn Arabic, and a great society of culture, learning, and coexistence (often called *convivencia*) flourished. For more than a hundred years, the Spanish city of Cordoba was the seat of the caliphs—

the supreme leaders of the Muslim world. Because of them, important books on medicine, science, and philosophy were brought to Europe. Cordoba's libraries grew to contain nearly half a million volumes.

With the gradual Christian "reconquest" of Spain, Muslims and Jews were at first treated with similar respect. The three cultures continued to live side by side. Muslims and Jews were still relatively free to practice their faiths. But they were subject to heavy taxes unless they converted to Christianity. Both Mudejares—Muslims living under Christian rule—and Jews were encouraged, and often forced, to remain in sections of cities enclosed by walls and guarded gates. New laws barred them from certain kinds of work, from marrying or employing Christians, from wearing fine clothes, and even from leaving their quarters on Christian holy days. They had to wear badges—in Castile, yellow for Jews, red for Muslims—so Christians would know "what" they were and be warned. The Crown and the Church claimed that Jews were constantly trying to convert Christians to Judaism, though there is no historical evidence to support this. In 1483, Jews were expelled from southern Spain.

Cordoba became a place of fear. It was now home to large populations of conversos: Jews who had converted to Christianity. Many had been forced to convert against their will—some upon pain of death. Others had chosen to convert for their own reasons, especially to stay in Spain. Spain—called *Sepharhad* in Ladino, the Spanish-Jewish language—was their new Jerusalem, their beloved home.

Encouraged by the Church, people began to turn against the conversos. A wild story spread that a converso girl had poured urine from a window onto an image of the Holy Mary in the street below. In supposed retaliation, hundreds of conversos were massacred. After that, the lives of the remaining Spanish conversos got much worse. They faced discrimination in their businesses and professions, in church, and in their everyday lives. They were often harassed or assaulted in the street.

Increasingly, the remaining Jews, conversos, and Mudejares were considered non-Spanish. The Crown and the Church, once seemingly motivated by a genuine desire to spread the Christian faith, now became obsessed with what they called "pure" Christian blood.

In 1481, the Holy Office of the Spanish Inquisition was born. Its purpose? To ferret out heresy against the Catholic faith. (Heresy is defined as a practice, belief, or even an opinion that doesn't conform to orthodox teachings.) Its practice? To arrest, torture, and punish every Spanish Christian even suspected of such heresy. It seemed the converted Jews had fallen into a trap. Now that they were legally Christians, the Inquisition could try them for not being Christian *enough*.

"Edicts of Faith" encouraged people to accuse their friends, relatives, and neighbors of heresy. "*Familiaris*" were chosen from the populace and appointed to spy and report on their fellow citizens. "Transgressions" as simple as refusing to eat pork (a Jewish dietary restriction) could get a person—and especially a converso—arrested. Thousands of people were burned at the stake at huge spectacles called *autos-da-fé.* And the Office's judges did not usually require proof. Those who held grudges could denounce their enemies for offenses that may never have happened.

So far, Mudejar subjects had not suffered the same persecutions, perhaps because there were powerful Muslim kingdoms to the south and east that might rush to the Spanish Muslims' defense. But the Inquisition, which confiscated the wealth of its prisoners, had made Castile rich. It could now afford to attack Muslim Granada, the third kingdom of the Spanish peninsula. It was the final piece of the puzzle in Isabella and Fernando's quest for a unified Christian Spain under their rule. The "Spain of the three cultures" was over. The war of the Holy Reconquest, as they called it, held the day.

conversos: A term used for Jews who converted to Christianity. They were also called **New Christians** and, sometimes, **Marranos,** which some historians think means "pigs" or "swine," perhaps an ironic reference to the fact that Jews and, allegedly, many conversos, don't eat pork.

Moors: This was the most common word used by the Spanish (and other Europeans) for people of the Muslim faith. It was often considered a derogatory term.

Moriscos: A word meaning "Moorish," which was used for Muslims who converted to Christianity.

Mudejar (plural, Mudejares): This was the Spanish word for Muslims who were living under Christian rule.

Old Christians: This term became more and more common as Spain became obsessed with "blood purity." True "Old Christians" were said to have had no Jews in their family history. After the Inquisition was instituted in Spain, many jobs and societies required documents proving that a person's family had been Old Christian for at least seven generations.

ONE

Ramon

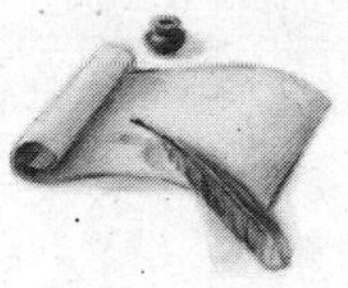

Cordoba, Castile

1485–86

Papa's Credo for Scribes

A scribe does much more
than just copy words.

He makes worlds
come alive.

Take pride in your art.
Take care.
Take your time.

A good scribe is a pitcher.
A pitcher holds wine
and spills not a drop.

That is how scribes
must treat words they take in.
Look at them closely.
If you miss even one,
it is gone. Maybe for good.

You must also be careful
of what you pour out.
Your hand must be steady.
Avoid what will shake it.
Wine itself—that is one thing.
Chasing girls is another.

"And if the pitcher
develops a crack?" I ask.

"Then it's of no use," says Papa.
"Don't worry. See here!"
Holds out a hand, slightly shaking.
"Sixty years old and never a tremor."

I try to laugh with him.
But we both know his whole
blessed body's been shaky of late.

Papa pretends not to notice
my worry. His grip on my shoulder is steady.

"Above all, Ramon,
you must always be true."

Our New Old Home

Cordoba.
It's been royal at least since the time
of the Romans. Even Hercules,
the great Greek, loved this city
of mine.

When the Moors conquered al-Andalus,
fair Cordoba, shut in by the Guadalquivir,
was the natural choice for their caliphate.
It became home to the head of all Muslims—
the caliph himself.

But the Moors were defeated a long time ago.
It has since been a jewel in the crowns
of our Christian kings. And now Isabella,
our gracious Queen, has arrived.
She's set up her court in the grand alcazar.
I can walk to its gates
in two thousand paces, plus thirty-three.

Amid all this glory, we Benvenistes
must eke out our days in the space
that was once used for servants.
Our stuffy rooms squat like beggars
deep in the heel of this house.

It's a fine house, you know:
as big as you'll see along this whole street.
But it's no longer ours.

When the Old Christians chased us
away from Cordoba, Papa said,
"There's no choice."
He knew of a place called Gibraltar.
We sold our fine house and ran
for our lives.

When we returned,
the house was still standing.
We were lucky—
few in our quarter still were.

But still standing, too,
was the man who had bought it.
He would not sell it back—
certainly not for the pittance he'd paid.

But he does rent us out
these four little rooms—
that's counting our shop—
for a handsome price.
Should we, I wonder,
be thanking God
for our blessings?

Why? During the riots
the whole of the city attacked
the New Christian quarter.
Hundreds of conversos—
people like us—were wiped
from the Earth.

I was just four. Mama tells me
we traveled by night to flee
Cordoba. By day, we hid.

Those who stood fast were attacked.
They were beaten with clubs.
With fists and stones.
One man we heard of
was dragged from a cart till he died.

So, why come back?
Good question.

We stayed just six months
in Gibraltar.
All Mama will say is,
"It didn't work."

It must have been bad
to be worse than this.
Now we're no more than servants
in our own home.

Fur

It's bizarre. I remember one thing
from the riots—so vividly
that it seems like this morning,
not ten years ago.

I am covered in soft, warming fur.
I think someone—an Old Christian
magician?—may have transformed me
into a rabbit.

I tell Mama this now,
my face burning. I'm fifteen!
What a babyish thing
to think you remember.
But I can't get it out of my head.

She gapes at me.
"Isidore," she calls,
"come and hear this."
Papa joins us.

Mama recounts it.
An Old Christian lady
saw us from her window.
We were crouched in a ditch.
Brave soul, she came out.
"Follow me," she whispered.

She hid us inside a vast trunk of coats
all that day, wedging *it* open
a crack for some air.

Well, all *I* remember
is the feel of fur.
They shake their heads.
"Isn't it—almost—quite funny?" asks Papa.
"'Changed into a rabbit!'"

We sit there and stare
at one another.
We can't seem to laugh.

The Scribes in Their Shop

Not every scribe
has such a small world.

Some books are made
by a whole troop of hands.

I've heard of a Bible, in Latin,
taking fifty-three masters a winter
to make it. (It was for the Queen).

Ten illuminators
just to draw and ink in
the gold-covered letters
beginning each page.

I'm not complaining.
I've come to like it this way.
Papa and I, bent over our desks.
We share tools, and a language,
and one enemy: the sun going down.

Mama can't really read,
but she helps.
Scrapes parchment with stone
so it's supple and smooth for our ink.
Sometimes she sets out the lines
for our letters. Her hand never trembles.

A quiet army of three: Papa, Mama, and me.
Six days in a week, I love it.
But part of me—perhaps it's the seventh-day part—
dreams a much different life.
Of knights, and explorers,
and of how in the world
I might ever become one.

Bookworm

Papa doesn't just love
the swoop and the swerve
of copying words.

Each morning he's up
before even the birds,
boring his eyes into books.

He must read every page
before it is copied.
Once we are through, the book
will sail back out the door—
and our lives.

Even ten years past *the times*—
that's what we all call the riots—
business is not, Mama says, what it was.
Though our days teem with words,
we can't afford to buy books of our own.

None of this makes Papa bitter.
Books are treasures, he tells me.
But their lives are fragile—
more fragile than wings
of dried butterflies.
Books have three of the deadliest foes
on this Earth:
fire, water, and ignorant men.
(Worms are bad too,
but they work more slowly.)

Still, books are the finest treasures of all.
You need only feast once with your eyes
and your heart.

And you'll be full with their wisdom
forever.

Cats

The world could ignite,
or turn pink, or end:
Mama and I would sleep
through it.

We're like cats in the sun.
We won't rise.
Not until we can bow
to our bowls of hot chocolate
and creamy goat's milk.

Papa makes breakfast,
then back to his books.
He shakes his head,
sad for us, as he goes.

I think it's a blessing,
this gift for deep sleep.
In Cordoba, churches and chapels
dot every street.
Ringing us round like a choker
with infinite loops of beads
within beads.

Each church has a bell
that sounds eight times a day.
There is matins at dawn, and lauds
sometime later, and then vespers
deep in the pitch black of night.

There are other names, too, that
I always forget. Papa says they mark hours
when the monks must say prayers.
But I think they're some kind of torture
the Church has devised. Either that
or they chime every time
some flea-bitten monk thinks of scratching
his head!

Fear

One dark dawn, I do wake.
A man like a mountain
is yanking the mattress
from under my back.

He mirrors the soldiers
who ride through my sleeps.
Sword at his side. On his cloak,
the lion and castle—the sign
of our good King and Queen.

The sheriff, says Papa.
Out for a thief
who's slipped from his grasp.

What is so precious
they feel they must shake
growing boys from their beds?
Mama is cross. She, too, has been woken.

Then I look. She is the one
who is shaking.

Justice

Days later, we hear it.
A boy, after all.
Much younger than me.
He wasn't yet ten.
Made off with a chalice,
plated with gold.
Small bounty at best.
But he hanged.

He was starving. An orphan.
Tried to trade it for cakes
in a town to the South.
There was him and his sister
and no food for their mouths.

The Queen advised mercy
on account of his age.
But this boy was a Jew.
Before she could stop it
he was strung up by men
of the sheriff's. All who passed through
the gate of St. James would see him there.

Beside him, the motto:
et justum es.
It is just.

When I hear about this
I remember that hand
creeping under my bed.

And sleep isn't easy,
for once. I lie in the dawn
and count sheep instead.

Confession

Most Jews left this place
ten years ago.
The Queen made it law:
every Jew in al-Andalus
must be baptized a Christian
or leave. Then followed those
four little words, favorites of queens:
on pain of death.

The few who defy her
hide in cellars and shadows
and caves underground.
I'm not really here. They have
less substance than ghosts.

The priests say the Jews
don't think Christ is God,
so they are our foes.
They're left on this Earth
to remind us why Christians are better.
We must shun them the way
we would shrink from the Plague.

Mama tells me all souls are equal,
at least in God's eyes.
Then says it's heresy
to argue with priests.
Do you doubt I'm confused?

I only know this:
we used to be Jews.

Baptisms

When a new bell is cast
and raised to its belfry,
it is baptized like a child.

The bishop anoints it with salt
and with oil. Then he pours
holy water over its metal head.

My great-great-grandparents
were baptized too.
They had as much choice
as one of those bells.
The riots those days, so I'm told,
were worse—far, far worse—
than the ones I've lived through.
The Black Plague was raging.
A third of all Europe died
from the sickness.
Fingers were pointed.
The Jews, it was said,
had poisoned the wells.

Not all were killed. Many Jews chose
to be baptized, to save themselves.
Others were held down by crowds
and given the rite no matter
their will.

So Mama's ancestors became Christians.
Even their surnames were changed.

And Papa's? My papa will speak
only of good—or should I say great.
How my great-great-grandfather
was a great, great scribe.
How he spoke and wrote Hebrew and Arabic
with more than just ease—with finesse.
By the end of his life he had served
a caliph and a king.

That end came too soon.
Mama told me.
Instead of baptism, my great-great-grandfather
chose death.
He took his own life, and the life
of his wife.

So which of these great ancestors
made the best choice?

Landlord

Señor Ortiz
is home for a spell.
I can tell by those stomps
on the ceiling, all day
and night.

He acts, says Mama,
like he's guilty of something.
As if he's afraid to take off his boots
in case he must run.

What from? I ask her.
But Papa says, "Raquel, shush.
How do we like it
when people talk rubbish
of *us*?"

Dinner Guest

Once a week—when he's here—
Señor Ortiz deigns to come down
and dine. Our table is humble,
but he doesn't mind.
He eats his plate clean every time.

I crave talk of adventures, and ships,
and exotic lands. Señor Ortiz
plies the coast of the Kingdom,
selling rich silks from the East.

But our landlord dislikes
my constant questions.
He's one of those people
who thinks children's voices
are irksome to God.

Whenever he's here, we have to eat pork.
I hate the stuff.
But it's the menu of choice
when company comes.

Eating pork is a sign.
It says you have left
being Jewish behind.
So good Christians must show—
whether they like pork or no—
that they can't get enough.

Edict of Faith

Today after Mass
we were required to swear
our allegiance once more.
That's the third time this year.

A huge crucifix was held
in the air by two priests.
We crossed ourselves, raised our
right hands. Swore to support and uphold
the Holy Office—as well as its agents on Earth.
The Inquisitors.

How, you might ask, does a peon like me
"uphold" the Office?
It's easy. It's all outlined
in the Edict of Faith.

They read it to us
every chance they get.
It goes on forever.
It speaks of transgressions that might
cost your life. Yet men fall asleep!

I can sum up the Edict
in one word: observe.

Neighbor, watch neighbor.
Friend, spy on friend.
If one of us errs,
we all suffer.
What to do then?
Tell Mother Church.
Don't worry your poor
little head about proof.
We'll believe you.

Heresy is a plague
and it spreads through people's souls
like fire through straw.

Don't let the small things escape you.
Does brother change to clean clothes
near the end of the week? That's a sign.
He's observing the Saturday Sabbath:
the day of the Jews.
Does sister refuse to eat pork?
That's a sign. She's following
old Jewish laws about food.

Does cousin cross his fingers behind him
while praising God? Spit on the ground during
Mass? Seem to smile when the Holy Virgin—
her statue—goes past?
Sign, sign, sign.

These people's souls are crying in need.
You must save them.

Better to burn here on Earth
than be lost to the hellfire forever.

Commission

Pigs' *feet* this time.
I never thought supper
would end!

Plates finally empty,
the table is cleared.
Papa brings out one book
we do own outright—the record
of all our accounts in the shop.

"Why so much credit?" whines Señor Ortiz.
You see, besides owning the house,
he is now partner in the shop.
So he says what he likes.

He thinks we've no talent for money.
And I must say, he's right.

If someone can't pay,
we'll copy for pies, or for paper,
or for some future favor.

Papa says good comes around
in the end. But there aren't
enough turns left in the Earth
for people to pay back what they owe us.

By the time the señor stands to go,
Papa's brow is down near his nose.
There's good news: our landlord sails
for Lisbon tomorrow.
And he's left us a job.
"One that pays," Papa says with a smile.
Or is that a grimace?

It's a stupid how-to for ladies at court.
How to dress. How many cloves
will cure rancid breath. How—
I'm not joking—to hold in your farts.

The patron needs fifty copies. By week's end!
So you see what's become of my art.

House Break

I've done nothing but copy
for days.

(Well, yes, on Sunday, we *did* break
for church.)

Each night when light fails
we must cease our labors.
Parchment's too precious to risk candle flame.

Our work at an end, I want to escape.
But since they hanged that young boy,
Mama and Papa prefer I stay in.

I've nothing to hide.
We are good Christians.
We keep all the fasts.
Who in this world would waste time
to hurt me?

One night, I can't stand it.
It's a feast day. Curfew is lifted—
for all but Ramon! I can hear the fiesta
from here. The streets sound alive
with people and song.

An ear to the door—
they're asleep. It's not hard to tell.
Both Mama and Papa snore like wild boars.

Free!
No thought to direction. I run.

All roads lead to the river: the Guadalquivir.
I'm there before long.
The water wheel's idle, but still I can hear
soft patters of splash. And then,
a girl's giggle. A boy's coaxing voice.

Are such moments for me?
Or will I go to my grave
having held in my hands
nothing softer than pages
made from cowhides and sheepskins?

Sabbath

Sundays, I am allowed out of doors for,
as my parents put it,
"a few hours of play."
You'd think I was five, not fifteen!

And even this freedom—a product
of fear.

If, on Sundays, you stay in your house,
the friars will think
you have something to hide.

Are you working in there?
Perhaps eating meat?
Both are forbidden on the Sabbath.
They're for secret Jews, and heretics.
Such monsters must burn.

So Sundays, it's safer outside than in.

Next Easter, there is to be
a royal joust. Though it's many months off,
the boys in the quarter think of
nothing else.
We practice with great concentration,
as if there's a chance we'll be knighted
tomorrow and asked to compete.

Our lances are branches
we've stripped from a tree.
But with my pumice stone
I sharpen their tips, just a bit.

Lope is taking things too much
to heart. Manuel has him down
and shouts, "Die, Jewish dog!"

Lope springs up as if scorpion-stung.
"Don't you dare call me that, you—
Marrano pig! Your mouth stinks of garlic,
the food of the Jews!"
"Well, *you* just plain stink!"
And that does it. The retort is so feeble
we all three start laughing.

But later that day I remember their faces
and long for sunrise.
To get back to work,
where words are safe.

Dinner Guests

They don't always leave
the spying to us.

One Friday, three men
storm in as we sup.

Fridays are fast days:
no Christian eats meat.

They peer into the pot
with such somber scowls,
I swallow a laugh.

It's only fish.
You can see they're upset
it's not adafina—Jewish meat stew.
Or—better yet—the head
of a bishop or two.

Then they leave.
No Goodnight or God Save You or even
a grunt.

Sliding

I've heard whispers.
Some New Christians err.
"Backsliding," it's called.

They may hide Jewish objects—
menorahs or prayer shawls, perhaps—
in their homes.

Or maybe they light candles on Fridays,
to prepare for a Saturday Sabbath—the choice
of the Jews.

And they might say, "Dio," not "Dios," meaning:
only one God.
That's Jewish too.

My parents don't do
any of this.
They are good Catholics.
Mama prays to the Virgin
even when no one is there
to take note.

But—
In the tiny, dark room
where both of them sleep,
there's a hole. You can't see it
unless
you know where to look.

I know.

I went past one night.
I heard a faint scrape.

Looked through the keyhole.
I wish I had not.

Papa was crouching down near his bed,
replacing a stone in the wall.
His movements were careful, as if
he were sliding a delicate loaf
of fine bread into an oven.

Perhaps the stone had come loose.
He was just mending it.
It is, after all, a very old house.
But my heart tells me no.
There is something inside
the recess in the wall.

The scariest part?
Because of that Edict of Faith
we pledged to at Mass,
I'm under oath
to find out just what.

Shoes

Father Cuesta, our priest,
is gone from the church!
A new man, Father Perez,
preaches the sermon.
He's stiff as a shirt
that's been dried in the sun.

The rumors are flying.
They say Father Cuesta,
a converso, you see,
was praying with Jews.
And not only that:
he wore, so they say, the communion host—
the incarnate body of Christ—in his shoes!

The new Father listed
the tortures of hell.
I peeked at Papa.
I know hellfire and demons
aren't things he believes.

I heard they pulled off his shoes in the square.
Father Cuesta's, that is.
Two bloody circles, red on white, were in there.

He swore they weren't hosts.
He'd given his *life* up to God:
why would he want to torture his son?
The circles of white were just
morsels of cotton to ease his sore feet.

So they said he was blistered
from going barefoot on *Pesach*,
the Passover fast of the Jews.

Poor Father Cuesta.
(He's sentenced to burn.)
The moral is this:
you're doomed if they start
to think of your shoes.

Guilds

I'm not your best guide
to how these things work.

All I know is you sure can't avoid them.
There are guilds for every Cordoban trade—
or just about. Guilds for breadmakers.
Guilds for blacksmiths. Guilds, even,
for cleaning latrines
where men shit.

From what I can tell,
these guilds are like clubs.
They have meetings and rules.
There are fees.
What's most important,
at least so it seems: each guild
has its own robes for processions.

We haven't had a guild in a while.
But things are changing. There is talk
of a printing press coming to Spain.
Scribes will lose work. They must organize.

That's all well and good.
I like fancy clothes.
Yet that's not all there is to the rumor.
Guilds are known for prizing *pure blood.*

There'll be no parades
for conversos like us.

Sure Enough

The guild of the parchmenters
is well established.

Its members have heard
of this new guild of scribes.
And been persuaded the guilds
must work together.
Business is business.

The short of it is, they've been told
not to sell us their wares.
Parchment must be saved
for true Christian scribes.

And we're not true Christians?
Do they think we mix our
"Jewish blood" with the ink
in order to write invisible lies?

Papa is livid.
What will we write on, our foreheads?
A scribe without parchment, he says,
is just like a voice
in a world with no ears.

Baptisms (2)

Here's what I don't get.
They once were obsessed
with baptizing Jews.

My ancestors did what they wanted.
Those of us who remain
are all Christians now.
There is barely a Jew left in al-Andalus.

Why do they hate us so,
still?

Auto-da-fé

I dream that flames kiss
my kneecaps.

Or a man strangles me
while a crowd shouts for blood.
Peace be with you, Benveniste!

But most often I dream of the man with the eye.
He was strangled before he was burned—
out of mercy. In the end, he'd repented.

But his eyes remained open.
We stood and watched.
When the flames reached his head,
you couldn't see much.
His hair, catching fire, haloed smoke.
Yet after a while I did notice something
dropping to the ground.

We were far back in that crowd.
By decree, the whole of Cordoba was there
to witness the spectacle.

In the dreams, though, the eyeball returns in
horrid detail.
It's as close as a pea might be,
on my plate.

Little Lies

When I wake from these dreams
I am sweating and shouting.
Mama hears and comes in.

She is angry, I know.
Not with me. At the fact
we're all made to watch
these foul shows.

Yet she consoles me.
We even try
to make it a joke.
"Did you see the eyeball?" she'll ask me.
"Was it red and bloodshot from his drinking
too much for his last hurrah?"

Once or twice I have woken in tears, like a child.
Mama tells me, those times, that I'm safe.
We're all safe.
Everything will be fine.

She knows I don't really believe it.
Neither does she.

But there's something amazing
about those bland words.
Those little lies that claim
our lives are normal.

To say them, to hear them,
feels gutsy. It's as close
to rebellion, maybe,
we will ever come.

Parchment

Now Yuce Tinto is gone!
No one has seen him
for one month at least.
Not even in church.

He is the man
who sells us our parchment.
He has a kind heart.
His prices are always
too cheap by half.

Papa sends me. Yuce
has no wife. Maybe he's ill,
helpless in his bed.

No one's there.
His home's been ransacked.
Shreds of parchment and paper
lie strewn like plucked feathers
all over the floor.

Everything points to the Inquisition.
Yuce, too, is a converso.
And I once heard him say
that Jews and Muslims can
go to heaven, if they are good people.

Who knows to whom else
he's said such rash things?
Poor Yuce.
He had a big mouth—
and many friends.
Both spell danger.
But together…

Mama cries when she hears it.
"What will become of that poor,
gentle man?"

I'm selfish. Our one source for parchment
has just disappeared.
Without it, we can't do our work.
So it's like we've no food.

What will become, my poor, gentle Mama,
of us?

Collecting

First, it was dead butterflies.
For a while, Roman coins
I'd find in the earth.
But *this* type of collection?
It doesn't suit me.

At long last, I can roam
through these streets. Yet I'd rather
be home in my room.

No one likes to pay debts.
Not even clients who once mussed my hair
and brought me sweet treats.

They make promises.
(Those come cheap.)
One gives me a barren old hen
in exchange for a prayer book
that took eight days to copy.

I pass by the mansion
of Don Barico.
He owes nothing.
In fact, he always pays in advance.
Often he'll even add wonderful gifts.
Plump partridge pies.
Candied almonds. Soft leather covers
for books.

I sigh. The word *candied* haunts me
all the way to our door.

Gift I'm scarcely inside
when I hear a knock.
There stands Don Barico himself,
as if he's been conjured
by my wishful thoughts.

But what twisted magic is this?

There's no partridge pie in his arms.
Instead, at his side, stands a boy.
Well, I think he's a boy.
There's a thin line of hair
just above his top lip.
(There's more above mine.)

But the rest of him—lost
in a mountain of cloth.
His robes touch the ground,
hiding even his shoes.
His hair in his turban could be
long or short or painted magenta,
for all I can see it.

There are two things, though,
you can't miss.

On his robe, just below his right shoulder,
the red patch of the Moors.

Above it, on his cheek, a black *S*.
Inked or burned, I can't tell,
right into his nut-colored skin.

Don Barico hasn't brought us a present.
He's brought us a slave.

Monkeys

I love Mama's laugh.
And God knows, it's a rare enough creature
these days.

But this time, it's wrong.

"Look at them stare at each other," she says.
"Like two nervous monkeys
peering over their barrels!"

No, *I* was just looking, not staring.
He's the one who won't quit.
Like I'm the strange one.
The stranger.

We Are Four

Never mind what we'll do with a fourth mouth
to feed
when there's barely enough for ourselves.

What will we do with two more working hands?

No commissions, no parchment,
not even much ink.

Plus, he's another
person to fear.

I've heard of some slaves, malcontents,
behaving like spies.

One insult from their masters:
they run to the Office.
They tell the first tale, no matter how false,
to enter their minds.

Papa, it's true, is a master scribe.
As am I, for that matter.

Most masters have servants.

Who cares?

We've always done fine
on our own, thank you kindly.

Papa's no fool. It won't be a day
before he sends this Moor back.

Arabic "Amir is still learning
his Spanish, Ramon. You
must help him."

"Yes, Papa."

Ha.

My friends and I talk
about him
even though
he's right here.
Like speaking aloud
with a donkey around.

He looks at us, straight.
Sometimes he blinks
like a fly's flown too close.
But even *could* he decode
what we say, well,
aren't his ears
tucked too tight
in that turban of his?

Shoo

Mama and Amir
now rule the kitchen.

I brood by the hearth—
it's just me sitting here, so it hasn't
been lit—and try not to listen.

Even with Mama,
he doesn't say much.
But she doesn't give up.
She babbles on, drowning
his silence with streams
of her talk.

When Papa or I try to help
with the meals, she just shoos us.
We are clueless and clumsy.
But Amir can *do* things.

Well, wait till I tell
the boys in the quarter
he can cook like a girl!

Strut

Amir drops
the docility act
when we're out of doors.

Everyone knows he's our slave:
I've told them.
But he struts like an equal.
He holds his head high.

They all can see it.
This kid, Paco, said,
"He makes like he
is the master of *you!*"

Companion

One thing I'll say:
with Amir here, Mama and Papa
don't nag me as much about going out.

I know why. They think I can't
get into trouble
with him as their spy.

What do they fear? That I'll scale
the high wall of a convent
if I'm left alone?

We're sent to the market;
I choose a route so roundabout
I feel dizzy. (If I'm stuck
with this guy, I vow to have fun.)
Amir narrows his eyes
but says nothing.
What can he say?

The streets wind like serpents.
For some reason I think of
a story I know, of Hercules.
As an infant, he cast
a swarm of snakes from his cradle.

He must have owned slaves.
Did he permit them to walk
by his side, as I do?

Retort

We turn from some alley
(I admit it: we're lost)
right into their midst.
A long line of men in fine robes.

On their shoulders, a dais.
There, clad in silk, sits a tall Virgin Mary
just as if she were real, and a queen.

The men seem to glow in their pride.
Women stand alongside,
throwing petals of roses at the men's feet.
From a high window nearby
someone wails, *"Nuestra Señora!"*
Our beloved lady!
The voice is so full
of both sorrow and joy
it prickles my neck.

Then, out the side of one eye,
I see a swoop of cloth.
It's Amir, down on his belly,
lips to the ground.

This has been law since the Christians
won Cordoba back from the Moors.
All Muslims must prostrate themselves
when an image of Mary or Christ
proceeds past.

Amir stands.
He catches me staring.
"You kneel in your church,
do you not?" he asks.
His Spanish—I gawk—
is smooth as glass.

Questions

So it seems that Amir's understood
every word that I've said.

He tries not to smile
as I come to grips with his trick.
But there's the smallest of smirks,
like the spout of his mouth
has a minuscule crack.

Now, at the market,
he speaks to the merchants,
asking for this many olives (only a few)
or that much salt. (I can't say
I mind this: I hate to shop.)

But on the walk home
we say not a peep.

Of what could we speak?
What I most want to ask
I know I should not.

Why's he a slave? Did he steal something?
Kill?
Has he ever been sold
in a market himself?

How many times
has his back felt a whip?
Does a person—kind of like cramps
in your hands when you write—
get used to it?

Do slaves dread tomorrows?
Plan escape? Dream of death?

I make it a game. Imagine I'll ask him
whatever I want (though I won't).

By the time we are home
I've chosen two.

What do you hope for?
That's one. And the second:
what do you fear?

If I were a slave,
I think I'd fear nothing.
Sure, I would dread
every lash of the whip.

But dread and fear
are not the same thing.

What's there to fear
when you have nothing left?

Pupil After supper, the roles
are reversed.
I help Mama clean up,
like a servant.

I guess washing dishes is easy enough—
even for blockheads like me.

Papa and Amir sit out
by the fire.
(Yes, for *him*, it is lit!)

They scribble away
on two separate slates.
(Amir's got an old one
of mine. No, no one's asked
if I'd mind.)

What do they write?
What else but Arabic?

You see, our Moorish slave
is teaching Papa—master scribe—
how to write!

Mama must see me scowling.
"Try to be gracious," she scolds.
"He may be a slave,
but Señor Barico brought him here
for a reason. He was meant
as a gift to Papa.
A great one."

I nod, say good night.
(Is that gracious enough?)
But I think: Mama has lost
all her fine talent
for comforting me!

Pity Can it get any worse?
Now I'm pitied
by our slave!

"My language is so difficult."
He wears a kind smile.
"Many great men do not know it."

I see. He thinks I think less
of Papa for this.
But that's not the problem.

No one's thought to teach *me* Arabic.
So I think less of myself.
Can you blame me?

The Kingdom barely knows I exist.
And now I'm old rags
here in my own house.

Ache

And why Arabic?
What makes *it*
such a great gift?

Hebrew—though it might
get us arrested—
that I could see
Papa wanting to learn.
Hebrew is tied to us,
to who we are.

Is Papa so quick
to forget this?

Listen to them!
They're at it again.
Studying, reading.
Talking language stew.
Mama waits up, dozing
by the fire.

I retire, but I hear them.
Their sound makes a lump
down deep in my belly.
It feels like I've wolfed a whole bushel
of berries, rotten and soft.

Mark of the Slave

When Amir and Papa finish at last
with their work for the night,
Amir comes to sleep in my room.

Aren't slaves meant to sleep
on the staircase or something?

It's not that he snores.
In fact, he's *too* quiet.

And that thing on his face
gives me nightmares.

Night after night,
he lies the same way.
On his left side.
Cheek against sky.

So unless the night's shade
is blacker than pitch,
I can see that *S*.
It shines up from his face
like some dark star.

What manner of man
burned that mark?
A Christian? A Jew?
A slave-trading Moor?

Does it matter?

Most nights, the *S* is the last
thing I see before my eyes close.
And the first thing I see upon waking—

whether or not
I've opened my eyes.

Al-Burak

Amir and I walk to the well
at the end of our street.
A voice from the grate
of a high dark window.

"Hey!"

I look up. The sun blinds my eyes.

"Fly away, al-Burak!"

Should I defend him?
Is a master dishonored
by taunts to a slave?

A rock falls near my foot.
And a second.
Amir's far ahead.

The rocks, and the name, are for me.

It rankles.
We conversos are as used to rude names
as an ass is to slaps.
Marrano. Turncoat.
Jewish wolf in sheep's skin.

Al-Burak—that's—a new one.
I can't help it.
I like to know what I'm called.

It sounds Arabic. I'll ask Amir.
No, I won't.

A man in the market
called him *damned shit-skinned cur.*

He'd laugh to know I was irked
by this one little slur.

Proud

We don't speak a word
on the way home.

I try to act calm, but I'm not.
Water sloshes and jumps
from my pail like the drops are at sea
and abandoning ship.

The black cloud's above me
all through dinner.
Everyone's quiet.
It's clear they can see it.

"You're a fool," Amir says
as he helps clear the plates.
"Don't you know al-Burak
was a magical steed?

"It carried my prophet, Muhammad,
on its back up to heaven.
I myself would be proud
to be called such a thing."

That figures.
Amir is just proud to be—
well, Amir.

That's the difference, I guess,
between him and me.

But how can I be proud?
Amir may be a slave,
but he knows who he is.

Mean *You're a fool.*
I should slap him.

And he's wrong, besides.

Those boys didn't mean
I was some noble thing.

A thing, yes, but not noble.
What they meant was:
I'm half like one creature, half like another.
A monster, therefore.
Such as: half-dragon, half-horse.
Half-woman, half-wolf
(I think Hercules
slew at least one of those).

Half-Christian, half-Jew.

Half-human.

At best.

Two Gifts

Papa journeys to Toledo.
I try to persuade him
he should take me. Everyone knows
bandits haunt the roads.

He refuses. I sulk.
But all is forgiven
upon his return.

He's brought gifts!

Mine is a knife: not just any.
Its blade is fashioned from Toledo steel—
the finest in Spain.

He's also brought back a gift for Amir.
But it's only a book.
How can *that* match a dagger,
especially for us? The air in this shop
is choked up with ink.

Papa sees my thoughts.
"It's not *any* book, boys. Some
say it's magic.
It can help you see truth, or
the future.
If you ask Hafiz something,
his poems will answer."

Hafiz is the author.
"Let's try it," I say.
"I've got one for him."

"O, Great and Potent Hafiz,"
(I'm hamming it up)
"which—the book or the dagger—
is the more precious gift?"

Amir shuts his eyes
and turns to a page,
pointing a place with his finger.

He plays with my patience.
What else is new?

At last he reads it.
He's smirking again.

How can two different eyes behold you as you are?
Each will see according to what it knows.

Just what I needed.
More answers that aren't.

Silver

Here's a question that,
when I heard the word *gift*,
flew out of my mind.
For a time.

How, when we're too poor
to add spice to our meat,
did Papa get presents?

Mama tells me.
A man in Toledo
buys all kinds of things.
Papa had something to sell him—
a set of silver Passover plates.

They had been in his family
for generations.
His mother, my nana,
willed them to him.

"Don't worry, Ramon," Mama says.
"It's okay. Better they go to his friend,
don't you think? All such things
will be taken from us,
in the end."

But Papa—carting that silver
on long, lonely roads,
alone on a mule
as slow as wet sand!
He could have been captured, or killed.

"I was just wondering—"
She cuts me off, smiling.
"You'd best limber up. Your hands
have grown flabby, and now work begins."

I soon learn what she means.
The book and the knife
aren't the end of the bounty.
He's also brought paper—
half my weight in it.

Silver (2)

To tell you the truth,
I feel like an anvil
that sat on my chest
has been lifted off
and thrown far away.

Those silver plates must have been
what was stashed
in that hole of Papa's.
And they're gone!

But why all that scraping?
It's clear why he hid them.
People are burned at the stake
just for having such things.
What I don't understand is,
why fetch them out from their cache
quite so often?
Was it for some ritual,
some heretic prayer?

Well, whatever it was,
it is over.

Unknown Nana, forgive me.
The plates may have been precious
to you,
and your memory.

But I'm glad they're gone.

Order

This job was worth
Papa's perilous trip?

The lovely, smooth paper
has come with a task that must fill it.

I should be rejoicing.
It's our biggest commission
in more than a year.

One *hundred* copies
of what's surely the dullest
book in the Kingdom.
It's called—are you ready?—
Native Plants of Castile.

I was angry, before,
when Amir shared
our scant work as scribes.

I've changed my mind.
For this job,
I will *graciously* take
any help I can get.

Auto-da-fé (2)

This one is different.
This time, no scaffolds
haunt the packed plaza.
No gigantic dolls—stand-ins
for men they can't find—
will hang from a tree.

The burning, this time,
isn't of flesh.

This is an *auto*
for criminal books.

A cache was found
in the walls of a *mikveh*—
an old Jewish bath.
Builders were razing the place,
making the way for yet
one more church.

Hundreds of books are wheeled to the square.
Monks yell at the carts like they're bad
little boys.

People jeer and guffaw
like they always do.
They warm their cold hands
in the flames of the fire.

But nothing is funny.
From the heaps glint the gold
of old Torah scrolls—the holiest
book of the Jews.

Papa's face is like stone.

Yet—there's a flutter
just under his shoulder.

His tunic moves
with the pounds of his heart,

like a curtain blowing
in a soft, killing wind.

Partners

When it's time for siesta
my hand is so cramped
from *Plants of Castile* I'd prefer
to poke out my eyes
than touch pen and ink.

Papa and Amir
see things differently.
Each siesta, they hole up
in Papa's room.
To "practice," they say.

One day there's a man
for Papa.
Just as I go to knock on his door,
the sound of my nightmares.
The scrape.

So it wasn't the plates!
The secret remains.
And Amir is deemed worthy
of having it shared.

I am not.

Again

Damn that closed door.
I try once more.
"What are they up to,
really, Mama?"

"They've told you, Ramon.
They're practicing."

Then I notice their slates.
There they are, stacked neatly
by the fire.

How can they practice
without slates to write on?
It's not like we have
any paper to waste!

Penitents

They pass day and night
clad in long, yellow robes called *sanbenitos*.

The penitents weep as they drag through the streets.
They call upon God for forgiveness.
Some flay their own backs
with cruelly barbed whips.
Blood spurts on bystanders
who don't seem to mind. It's said
blood shed in penance is holy.
Some even *try* to stand in its path.

But this, to me, is the creepiest part:
in his hand, or hers, each penitent
carries a candle,
unlit.

It's like a bad dream to have them around.
No one must greet them.
That's part of their sentence.

You might think they're lucky.
They have erred, yet they haven't been burned.
But their honor is gone. They'll never
again work at good jobs. And what money they had
has been seized by the Office.

Worst of all, when their sentence of weeping
and flogging is through, their *sanbenitos*
will hang on the walls of their churches.
Shaming their families forever.

Black If you *still* won't confess
under torture,
your garment is black.
That means you will burn.

What color would
Papa's *sanbenito* be?

Request Okay, he's surprised me.
I suspected Amir wanted nothing in life
but to kneel by Papa. To serve every whim
as a page serves a king.

But he's asking permission
to leave. Not for good. (No such luck!)
But for one afternoon
every week.

He wants to say Friday prayers
at the mosque across town.
Papa agrees, but pats the air
with his hands. That means he's upset.
Or, rather:
he's scared.

What if Amir makes new friends and talks
about what Papa has in that wall?
(He speaks in two tongues, after all!)

Or maybe Papa is scared *for* Amir—
for his safety.
The way he once worried
over only me.

You'll say that I'm feeling self-pity.
Am I not justified?

Sure enough, Papa says,
"Amir, you may go, but Ramon
must go with you."

So the master's been made
servant to the slave!

Shades of Blue

I take it all back.
Forget I complained.

May Allah be praised!
I like these Fridays.

Today a bona fide miracle
came down for this boy.
An angel made flesh.

The Mudejar quarter is tucked
in a corner of Cordoba
as if it is hiding.
Maybe it is.

No matter.
Today was the first truly warm
day this year. While Amir went to pray,
I lay on a rock by the Guadalquivir,
admiring the sky. What kind of blue?
Indigo? No. Cerulean?

Azure, I decided.
Don't be too impressed.
These are colors of inks!
Scribes can recite them
as effortlessly
as priests can count sins.

Shades of Blue (2)

I thought I knew blue.
I hadn't met *her*.

She was washing some clothes at the shore,
laughing and singing with three silly friends.

I made my way over.
In my best imitation
of a rich, courtly knight,
I bowed very low.
(For once, I am glad
of those how-to books!)

The girls laughed. But my angel
fixed me with her eyes.
Those don't need fancy nicknames.
They're simply, exquisitely,
blue.

She plucked a white flower from
behind her ear.
I have it here now.
Its softness is brittle,
like Egyptian papyrus, the plant
the ancients once used for paper.

The petals so light, they practically float
in my palm.
But the flower is here.
It's as real as a promise.

Divining

The *S* rises and falls
so evenly.
His sleep must be deep.

The book is Amir's.
I know that I'm risking
our thin, eggshell peace.
I feel like I stand
by the Guadalquivir,
knowing that I,
in a heartbeat,
could jump.

But I'm haunted.
Beatriz Alvarez.
That's her name.
The sounds of those vowels
can bubble my blood.

I must know this:
should I pledge her my love?
I know that I want to.
But how will she act?

Will she laugh in my face?

Amir keeps Hafiz tucked under
his thin square of pillow, just as a girl
might do with her doll.
There!
I have it.
He doesn't stir.

I sneak to a corner.
Squeeze my eyes shut.
A page near the middle.
My finger nests in.
Then his voice, from the bed:
"Next time, at least,
leave your feather pillow
behind as a trade!"

Code

I don't turn around.
I'll try to read quickly:
he'll soon snatch it up.

It's nothing but squiggles!

I roar at Amir.
"You slippery thing!
You never said
it was written in code!"

He's still wiping sleep from his eyes—
but his smirk is awake, you can bet.
"It is Arabic. The tongue
of my father—"

"I *know* what it is.
No one can think of anything else
since you came to this house!"

I make to storm out, then—
here's a new thought.
I grab his high collar.

"Teach me!" I shout.

For a heart-thumping minute
I think he might strike me.
I half wish he would.
For a slave to do that to a free man
means death.

Papa is there.
"Ramon! What is wrong?
It's not even dawn!
Why are you shouting
to wake up the dead?"

A Caution

The Arabic lessons
don't go very well.
The letters entwine, run together
like droplets of water.
They skitter and swim
from under my eyes.
These aren't the curves
I care for right now.

Amir won't give up.
I can tell that he's back feeling
sorry for me.

On none of our walks
have we seen Beatriz.

The Queen's royal joust
is two days away.
All of Cordoba, it's certain,
will come.

"What will I say if I see her?"
(I mean Bea, not the Queen.)

He fetches Hafiz. Offers it first,
as if after two weeks of study
I'll be able to read it.

I don't know whether to thank him or scream.
"You translate," I tell him, as grand as I can.
"The book's yours, after all."

Amir opens Hafiz
to a random page.
It takes him no more than a minute
to magic his language to mine.

Look not upon the dimple of her chin—
Danger lurks there!

"It doesn't say that! You're having me on."

Amir says nothing. Doesn't smile, doesn't frown.
He's harder to read than the words on that page.

Joust of Champions

Clang of armor,
clash of swords,
the rock-hard crush
of lance against
chest.

The old Ramon
lived for this stuff.

But the contest is not
what I'm here for.
I don't dare tear my eyes from the crowd.

The day is waning.
The prizes (one is a horse
clothed, head to tail, in gold-threaded
silk) have been given out.

Oh, how will I sleep?
I was so sure I'd see her.
Then, just as we're leaving,
a faint laugh behind me, cool water
on pebbles. I turn—
too late. No one is there.

Amir rolls his eyes
and points to my satchel.
Unfastened, as always.
A small sheet of paper,
as fine as I've seen,
lies planted in there like a seed.

There is no code.
This girl is direct.

She names the day, and the place.
Isn't the man
supposed to do that?

I don't care.
I could joust with the
champions now.

By this time next week,
we'll have met!

Señor Ortiz

Our landlord is back once again.

We hear his footstomps,
and the slide of his servant's
long cloak on the floor.

The two of them stay
locked up in those rooms
at the top of our house.
The best, brightest ones.

But they might as well be
down here beside us.
The air when they're home
becomes something else.
Something not ours.

Dinner Guest (2)

Amir comes in from the well
after washing his hands
and joins us at the table.
Señor Ortiz looks up and sees him.
He whistles air in through his teeth.
The sound is so ugly.
Like toenails on tile.

Papa declaims on the way it once was.

How the Muslims
ruled here for lifetimes.
Seven lifetimes, in fact.
Hundreds of years!

How their streets ran with fountains.
How they planted trees bearing fruits
no Christian had heard of till then.
How the libraries here in our very city
held many more books than the sky contains stars.
"Forty *thousand*, señor—Can you fathom that?

"Then we Christians, returning,
tore their babes from their arms and even
their bellies. It's still done today.
Amir here was snatched from his birthplace
and sold at a bargain to Don Barico
as if he were naught but maggoty bread."

Señor Ortiz throws down his spoon
with a crash. "Do not, Isidore,
preach history to me.
You cherish the old days,
and the old days are dead.

"We are at war, and you feed a snake
in *our* very own nest."

Words

The *Plants* man has decided
he needs twenty more copies
to take on his journey
to Aragon.

Why would the Aragonese
want to read about
every last leaf in Castile?
No one asks.
Each copy we make
is like one more meal.

But even Papa
is grumbling now.

"Papa," I ask him,
"why not write your own books?"

(He loves words, does he not?
He's always saying Thing A is like B
and Thing B is like C.
Why don't we copy *his* words
in the shop?)

Papa smiles at the ground
like a joke's inscribed there.
But after a moment
he's solemn again.

"Far better to copy well, and true,
than invent badly," he says.

How many times have I heard that by now?

I still think he should try it.
And I see that it warms him to think that *I* think
that he could.

Shake We have copied for so many hours on end
my hand's no longer a hand, it's a claw!

Even my initials look like they're done
by a child not yet ten.

It's not just the hours.
My hand won't stay steady.

I think of what Papa said of strong drink—
and girls.

I still water my wine, so I don't think it's that.
As for girls—

Well, it's true—I meet Bea tonight!

Clean

Mama frowns at my tunic.
What? It's my cleanest one.

"Turn around."

Ah—there's a spot after all.
(Dirt blares much brighter
in the presence of mothers.)

I can't see what she's doing,
but a force strong and wide

licks the length of my back—
a giant's rough tongue.

I turn around, startled.
Do I look like a floor?

"Close your eyes," she commands.
"There'll be dust." The broom scrapes

my front. My tunic is lined
with faint tracks of black.

"There. Now you're safe."
But she barks it.

"No one can say
that your clothing is clean

for the wrong blessed day."
Spins away.

The broom clatters down
like the jeering applause

at the *auto-da-fé*.

Near Perfect

Here we sit: me with Bea.
Bea—I can hardly believe it—with me.

Her hand rests on mine. Just lightly, as though
it's not really there.
But it's there!

Only the scent of the orange tree above us
proves I'm not dreaming.

Everything's perfect. Then—*greech!*
My stomach's near empty, as always.
(Would that the *Plants* man had paid in advance!)
In a sweet, silent moment, it gurgles and turns.
Then lets out an utterly *hideous* yell.

I try to ignore it. Not to mention the rich,
stirring scent of the tree.
(The fruit all belongs to the Crown.
I don't fancy losing this hand
to a lurking sheriff—just when I've got
Bea to hold it.)

Greech! Yet again.
All I can do is sit still and pray
that, among all Bea's perfections,
impeccable hearing's not one.

Jewels

Now that spring's here,
we get what we've longed for
all winter.

It's snowing!

People stand in the streets with their tongues
stuck far out and their noses turned up to the sky.

Jewels of pure cold land soft in our mouths.
They melt into memories
even before we can pin down their taste.

Our faces are wet from the flakes.

But before long I see—
Amir's is not drying.

Zero

"Amir, why not ask this Hafiz
where your parents are now?"

Amir shakes his head.

"And why not?" I insist.
"Come, let's try."

A face full of fire.

"You're so good with numbers,"
he says. "Don't you know about zero?
Take a cart full of zeros,
pile them into a mountain—
what do you have?
Still zero.

"Hafiz can shed light
on what's already there.
That is all.

"Now, *Master* Ramon," he says
with an angry toss of his head,
"please—leave me alone."

Raro *"Es raro,"* she says.
Strange.
I quickly learn how much Bea
adores that small word.

Everything's *raro*. The clouds in the sky,
shaped like roosters today. They're *raro*.
The girl over there, can't you tell that's a wig?
Doesn't she know those are sewn
out of dead people's hair? She's *rara* indeed.

Nearly all that we see
is judged in this way.
I don't quiz her on how this could be.
If everything's strange, then strange
must be normal. Correct?

One day by the river
a leper walks by.
We split from our kiss
at the jing of the bell at his neck.
We say it together. *Raro!*
And laugh, though
nothing's that funny.

I wonder, then on.

Does Bea know, guess, or fear
that I'm an al-Burak?
And if so, is *raro* the worst word
she'd use for me?

Fernando's Army

King Fernando departs with an army so vast
it seems to contain every man in the world.
It's hard to believe enough still remain
to make up this crowd.

Those like me—too poor to own horses
or swords—are left behind.
We cheer and clap.
Women throw garlands, wave handkerchiefs
that are dusted with scent. The air's thick
with perfume and the first heat of spring.

It's not fair.
"*I* should be going," I say.
Amir jabs me a look.
"Not, of course, to kill Moors.
Just to get out of this bloodthirsty place."

Amir shakes his head.
"And wars don't drink blood?"
But he doesn't sound angry.

He follows the soldiers
with faraway eyes.

A Cow, at Breakfast

No more hot chocolate at breakfast
for Mama and me. Try, instead,
a loaf left from Tuesday,
soaked in brackish warm water.
At least this way it's more
like a clump of wet sand
than tooth-splitting rock.

On the bright side, we'll soon, at long last,
see the spoils of those *Plants of Castile*.
On the dark, we don't have a clue
what we'll do next.

The mountain of paper brought back
from Toledo is now little more
than a bump.

Paper is less dear than parchment, it's true,
but that doesn't mean it comes cheap.
Papa says enough paper to fill just one order
costs almost the same as a very large cow.

Lying in bed, I play a new game.
Which one of the books in the world,
were it mine, would I trade for that cow?

Or, which *page* of which book
would I trade for a bite of fine beef?
Or even a hoof, or an eye,
or a tongue?

I could boil some nice leather covers
instead. Eat them as a soup.
That couldn't be worse
than this morning's bread.

What could?

The Apprentice's Masterpiece

Papa wanted to keep the line going.
He had only one child, one son—what else
should he be but a scribe?

Most families send out their sons
when they're seven or eight.
They live and apprentice with other
men, in other trades.
In exchange, the boy's parents
get a good little sum.

Well, I stayed home. I was glad.
What better teacher is there than Papa?

From every successful apprentice
a master is made.
To prove his mettle, the new master
must create—well, what else?
A masterpiece.

Papa wouldn't exempt me.
But he found me a book
that he knew I would love.

The Twelve Works of Hercules.
The stories are full of adventure
and places that I've never been.
Best of all, Enrique de Villena,
the man who composed it,
is Cordoba's very own son.

Each day, after closing the shop,
I copied till Mama insisted I stop
to eat dinner. It was always too soon.
The words seemed to fly from my fingers.
The work wasn't work.

At the end of a year, I had my
masterpiece. Its pages were perfect.
My quill never slipped.

I was so proud.
I couldn't stop turning its pages.
Admiring the slant of my letters,
the fine, feathered strokes
of the ink.

And now it's been almost
two years since I've touched it.

What if I sold *Hercules*?

Here it sits, worthless, under my bed.
Shouldn't it feed my family
instead of just fleas and rats?

Bestseller

The Edict of Faith
has been read again.
The Father advised us
to look to the chimneys
of known conversos.
If we see smoke on Fridays,
we must denounce those
who live in that house.

Despite all this madness
there are one or two people,
very brave souls, who haven't stopped
all their business with us.
I know without asking
they want it kept quiet.
When their work is ready
I slink to their shops as if carrying tracts
by assassins.

One of these men is Señor de Allende.
He's an Old Christian—his seal of pure blood
is framed on his wall.
But he's always shown nothing but kindness
to us. He's my first stop.

When I reach his street,
I can hardly get near
for the press of the crowd.

Though few can afford to eat meat
in these times of drought, they're lined up
like sheep
for this latest new thing.

A week's wage for the very same book
all their neighbors will buy and learn off by heart.

Al-Burak: Why Conversos Are Devils.

Hercules and I will have to come back.

Commission (2)

Father has sent a new patron away!
I'm so angry, I turn—
nearly yell at my father.

He is crying. This is a sight I refuse
to get used to. Yet lately, I do.

Again—poor Papa—it's over a book!

"That, my Ramon, was an *exquisite* thing."

"A trap." Mama's face
is nut-hard, furrowed
with new lines of frown.

"I don't think so, Raquel. Still—
I'm sorry, Ramon. How I'd love you to work
on something that fine. Then would you see
the true depth of our art.

"It was a Passover prayer book, a fine *Haggadah*.
One of the few Jewish books in al-Andalus
not consumed by their fires."

Mama says, "Isidore, don't have second thoughts.
If they found out you'd so much as touched that
one book,
they'd call it backsliding.

"Think of Ramon.
If they burned you for work
you'd chosen to do, wouldn't they take
your apprentice too?"

Backsliding

Were the choice mine, I'd do it.
I would copy that book.
I would take that bold chance.
But when is the choice ever mine?

As for that ladder, that great, famous ladder
to Christian from Jew,
I don't recall any such thing.
How can I slide down
what I never climbed up?

You know what?
I don't recall ever taking one step
that wasn't mapped out for me first.

Knives

I look, really look,
at my mother. It must be
the first time I've done so
in months.

I feel a cold shock.
Could this be the pillowy Mama
who once scooped me up
like I weighed nothing more
than a glove?

Now the bones at her collar
jut out like stashed knives.
Her skin looks too thin,
like parchment rubbed free
of a thousand mistakes.

Return

Señor Doda is here.
He's been coming to us
since before I could write.

Now he's here to return
the last book that he ordered.

"It's paper!" he says, to explain.
"My wife believes only the Jews"—
here, he cringes—"use such things."
He smiles, turns his hands
so the palms face the sky.

"But paper is better than parchment, señor,"
I tell him. "They've used it in China
for hundreds of years."

Señor Doda won't be swayed.
"What if I wanted to sell it again?
My wife's not alone in her thinking.
No one will touch it.

"I'm sorry, Ramon.
But I won't be allowed
back inside my own door
if I pay you for this."

The *Familiari's* Daughter

Bea's angry. At me.

I've failed to notice
something about her.
(It seems hard to believe.)

I wheedle. "Give me a clue."
She scowls, but relents.
"Oh, you'll never guess, you ignorant boy.
It's my skirt. Can't you tell? It's fine
Persian silk. A thousand times finer
than that old sack I wore!
A blind man could see it."

I appease her. I tell her
her own perfect beauty
blocks everything else.
She warms up.
(Once again, those daft books
pay off for Ramon!)

I know that it's rude
to inquire about money.
But we Benvenistes have so little—
it's made me obsessed.
"So…what is the source
of this new gush of wealth?"

She claps her small hands, so glad I've asked.
Her father's been named *familiari*.
A familiar, a spy, of the Inquisition.
There are riches, it seems,
in ratting on friends.

I pretend to be thrilled.
But what I'm thinking instead:
Aren't people like him
in the business of squashing
conversos? People like Papa, and Mama,
and me?

Green

Bea invites me to lunch at her home.
She says, "Only my mother and sisters will come."
Only?

I feel, by the end,
as if I've been grilled
by Inquisitors—four of them.

But the food!
Warm bread and plump olives. Long, thin
slices of serrano ham, marbled red and white.
More food than I've had for two solid weeks.
But the ham, slippery as it is,
seems to stick in my throat.

Later, Bea asks, "Was lunch not to your liking?
Though you ate like three men, your face
was as green as the olives."

"It's just—"
I don't want to insult her.
"My parents—we rarely eat pork.
It's so costly, you know," I hasten to add.

The minute it's out,
I want it back in.

Bea stares. Those luscious lips gape.
Take care, I should tell her, or you'll swallow bugs.
I cover my panic
with an awkward kiss.
She at first pulls away.
And then
she returns it.

Heirlooms

After lunching at Bea's,
I see our small rooms
with new eyes.

Though Bea's house is three times
the size of our place,
it is ten times more cluttered.

Theirs is filled up with objects.
Paintings and vases. Carpets
and crests.

All of it seems very old.
Much of it bears the Alvarez crest.
One thing is certain:
there's no mistaking
whose house you're in.

Our home is tasteful and, thanks
to Mama, always clean.

But what do we own
that says who we are?

Poem Amir seems to think I'm out of my mind.

"Where have you been? Do your eyes see nothing?
This is no time for roses and moons!"

Is he jealous? Bea's pretty. Has he kissed any girl?

I can't tell you why, but I want him to like her.
His scorn is a fly in my cup full of wine.
"Come on"—this will get him—
"Help me write her a poem."

He narrows his eyes. "As you will," he says, soft.
"Bring me your slate."

Here's what he writes.

Your lips are as red
as the blood on the hands
of your father.

"That will fire up her passion,
Ramon, don't you think?"

Edict of Grace

Over the course of one month,
explains Father Perez,
we are invited to tell on ourselves.
For these thirty days, punishments
will be several shades lighter.
Now is the time
to come clean to the Office.

The queue the next morning
at the alcazar
winds through three streets.

Papa tells us of the last
such Edict of Grace.
People owned up to things
they'd not *dreamed* of till then,
let alone done.

What's the catch?
Well, for one thing,
although they don't burn you right then,
they do record all that you say
in their file. It will be there
if—or, when—you err again.
Repeat offenders
don't fare so well.

For another, they fine you.
The Church coffers bulge
from the fantastic tales
people spin for the Grace
just to keep themselves safe
—so they think—
in the future.

One more thing: they won't let you go
till you rat on others.
"Surely," they'll say, "you
did not act alone in these things
that you did? Don't hold your tongue.
We know that you live in the world,
and have eyes.
What more can you tell us before you go home?"

Ink

Back from Friday prayers
with Amir. We dawdled.
Papa will scold us,
I'm sure.

I'm wrong.
His mind is elsewhere.

"Papa," I ask,
"are you unwell?"

He says not to worry—
he was just resting. Sleep, he says,
still clasps him by one hand.

His nice turn of phrase
draws my glance there.

We've finished the last
of the work that we have.

And yet Papa's fingers
are stained with fresh ink.

Garrucha Manuel and Lope know all the tortures.

Prisoners, if released,
must swear solemn oaths
not to say what they've seen.

But Lope's uncle is *involved*
with the Office. He loves
to scare ladies at dinner
with gory details.

Lope favors one called the *garrucha*.
The accused hangs
by the wrists from a pulley.
Heavy weights are attached
to his feet.

They raise him up slowly.
Then let him fall
with a jerk.
His arms pull out
of their sockets.
And sometimes
his legs.
Lope assures us
it really hurts.

He adores nothing more
than acting this out.
He dangles from trees,
piercing the air with fake screams.
Lope's a strange boy.
He and his uncle
must surely be cut
from the same bolt of cloth.

Sure It *must* be a book
inside Papa's wall.

One that leaves tired hands
spotted with ink.

Is he writing something, then,
after all?
Does it contain things
he could burn for?

Why don't I sneak in
and see for myself
rather than twisting my brain
into knots?

Because. What if I knew,
and then was arrested?

I am weak.
How would I withstand
the *garrucha*?

To condemn my papa
with my cowardice—
I couldn't take that.

So my arms and kneecaps
go dead with terror
each time I creep near his door.

Papa, your secret is safe—
if only from me.
I can't go in.

Condition

I'd wondered, of late,
why the footstomps above
had shushed to a halt.

We'd known Señor Ortiz
was still in the house.
His fine horse is there
when I pass by the stables
in Trinidad Street.
His servant still shuffles about
in señor's bedroom.
I know, for it's right above mine.

But lately the house has felt
like it's waiting

And now comes the letter.
Señor Ortiz has the dreaded Smallpox!
He may die.
He dances already
on Death's ashen palm.
All the Reaper must do, now, is choose.
Should he, should he not, close
his strong, bony fingers and squeeze?

We're astonished:
if señor dies, says the letter,
the house will be ours.
As well as the shop.

There's a condition.
We must show loyalty
to our Queen and King.

We must, says the letter, cast *the Moor* out.
If we're to go on having a home
Amir must once more have none.

Too Long!

Papa goes up
to *reason*
with him.

Mama says it takes reason to reason,
and Señor Ortiz, sadly, has none.

Papa's not daunted.

"I'm every bit as unreasonable
as he is," Papa says.

That's a good thing?

And is it reason
to spend hours in a room
with a man who has Pox?

One more bell
has just sounded.
Time marches on.

Will my ox-stubborn papa
never come down?

Señor's Answer

is no.
Papa says
we must think
about where we might go.

He mentions Granada.
Amir's eyes light up.

I, too, feel a pang.
Haven't I dreamed
of seeing the world?

But this is our home.
And travel takes strength.
Does Mama have it?
And Papa?

Señor Ortiz is changing his will.
This whole house—the house, might I add,
that used to be ours—will go to the Church!
You know what that means.
The Inquisitors.

If he dies, Papa says,
they'll be here to lay claim
before señor's body
is put in the ground.

They've arrested so many New Christians
of late. Even I, who love numbers,
would not want to count them.

The Queen's alcazar
can't hold them all.
Some people wait years
before their trials start.
Waiting takes space!

Once, when I wasn't permitted
to do what I pleased,
I said my own room
was a prison cell.
Had I glimpsed, without knowing,
the dark final fate of our home?

Question Mama and Papa talk half the night.
Amir's awake too.

I have a new question
to ask Amir.
How does it feel
to throw your kind master
out of his home?

Front Door

Most people who call
on Señor Ortiz
know to use the back door.
The front one is ours.
(In my grandfather's day,
it belonged to the servants.)

This doctor is not from our quarter,
and he doesn't know.
Or maybe he's not all that keen
to be seen.

He wears no strange hat
like the ones in old books.
But his beard is as long
as his arms.
Nearly hidden beneath it,
just right of his heart:
a yellow patch.

He's a Jew.

If *they* learn he has been here,
Smallpox will be
the least of our woes.

Penitent I still meet with Bea.
My world may be ending,
but that only leads me
to think of her more.

I even remember to compliment her.
I look for silk, for gold thread—
any small thing that I might have missed.
But the skirt is the old one!
This sack, she had said.

Girls are confusing.

"Don't look at my clothes!"
She's noticed my gaze. "I'm ashamed!"

It takes much kissing and coaxing
(not that I mind)
before she'll explain.

"Mama confessed for the Edict of Grace.
She told them she once bought some meat
from a wandering Jew.
They fined her three hundred maravedis,
and Papa won't pay. He says
we must sell off our new clothes instead!
Oh, Ramon—I wish I were dead."

But couldn't he stop it? He's a *familiari!*

She looks at me like I am simple.
"My *father's* the one who said,
'Turn yourself in.'"

She dabs at her eyes for a minute.
But when she looks up, they are slits.
"You know, Ramon,
maybe he was right.
If ever again there's an Edict of Grace—
Better to tell on yourself
than be told on.
I'm sure you've done *something*.
No, don't tell me.
Tell *them*."

Waiting

We wait for señor to die
or to live.

Papa once claimed that waiting
is food for the soul.
Think of a pen, he told me.
When a new one is made,
we must stand it in sand
to strengthen the feather.
After one week of patience,
the quill is more pliant.
Less likely to break.

I'm sorry, Papa, but some waiting
just leads to despair.

What's more, it costs money!
It's hardly fair.
Why, when there's nothing to do,
do we still need to eat?

I go looking for work.
The doors in the quarter
are lids on sealed coffins.
In other words,
shut.

I'm not choosy.
Amir's washing clothes
for Señora Ducal.
I must find something too!
I can't let the pennies
earned by our slave be what feed us.

At last, near the end
of a dark crooked street,
a door is swung open.
There stands a grizzled old man
as spindly as a broom.

He looks me over
through a fearsome squint.
Then he spits.
The hands that killed Christ
will never be clean.
He sticks out his chin as he says it.
Spittle lands
in my wide-open eye.

Get out of here, Jew.

Tail

It's as if
I'm walk-
ing around
with horns—
devil's horns—
in place of
my ears.
Or a tail
instead of
no tail.
It's invisible,
but might
spring out
hey-ho!
at any
bad moment.
Of which
there is
hardly a shortage,
these days.

I'm more angry
than scared. I've
done nothing
wrong.

But in this time
and this place
that particular
armor is thinner
than paper.

Stain I must do something.

If we seem like Jews
to some half-blind old man,
how long will the Office
leave us alone? They say
they deal only with Christians.
But then they say Christians
are more prone to *err*
if their blood is unclean.

We don't boast about
our Jewish ancestors.
We bury our pride
deep down in our hearts.

There must be something.
Some mark or some stain
that singles us out.

They will come looking.
Every last thing that they see will be judged.

Even if that book Papa hides
is no more than a clandestine copy
of *Plants of Castile*, they're bound
to find something else.

In Seville, a man burned for saying
that God and Allah are the same.
I've heard Papa say things more shocking
than that! Mama, as well.

And what about me? I don't study
the Edicts of Faith like I should,
so I don't know what not to do.
I could be arrested for anything—
for picking my nose
with the incorrect finger!

Guides I have an idea.
A way to save, all at once,
Papa, our home,
and even Amir.

But it scares me.

I remember one thing
from the Edict of Faith.
No Christians may use Jewish doctors.
Even a potion that's sold by a Jew
might as well be a poison—so sure a ticket
is it to a *very* good seat at the *auto-da-fé*.

What if Señor Ortiz
were arrested?

I scare me.

There are two angels appointed
to each man on Earth.
A good one,
to protect him.
And a not-so-good one,
to sometimes put him
to the test.

Which of my angels
is singing
right now?

The Alcazar

Come back in a fortnight?
They must be mad!

It's not just that I've wasted
all day in that line.

It took all the courage I had
to lift up my fist
to their door.

On Second Thought

Here comes that broom-man.
Shrink, Ramon, into this wall.

He doesn't see me,
or, if he does, looks
right through.
As if I am a window
in a fancy new home,
covered, but only with glass.

Instead, he starts shouting
at Señora Monzon. She's as pure
an Old Christian as there is
in Castile.

The man shows his fist.
"Get lost, you Jewess!"
The señora ignores him.
A man passing by on his horse only laughs.

"You crazy old bugger," says this hidalgo.
"You see Jews in the very
blades of the grass!"

So... So,
it seems I overreacted.

True,
Señor Ortiz will probably die—
few survive the Smallpox.
I would never have come up with that plan
if that weren't the case.

Still,
death doesn't stop
the Inquisition.
At every *auto-da-fé*
I've seen people long dead
burned at the stake.
They dig up their bones
for the purpose.

I suppose it is better
than burning alive.
But death is sacred, I think.
No one deserves
that kind of last shame.

So,
I'm doubly glad that,
when I went there
to rat on señor,
they sent me away.

Yet,
something nags.
Before the clerk said
to return in two weeks
he asked me my name.

I did not see him write it.

Or,
I might have.
Did I?

My mind is a haze
of panic
and regret.

Pledge

Bea says that for making a pledge,
there's no better time than the worst.

I *think* that means
she might love me.

I must meet her this Friday.
The cathedral courtyard.
We'll bind our friendship
(as she calls it)
by exchanging gifts.

Might this be the time to come clean
that I'm poorer than mud?

She reads me. "I don't care what it is—
just make certain it's the best
thing you have."

I'm relieved.
That lasts for a blink.

"Don't disappoint me, Ramon.
Lots of boys with blood purer than yours
would jump in the Guadalquivir
for the chance to be mine.

"You don't want to see
my side that's not sweet!"

Doctor

That doctor calls Señor Ortiz
our "patron."
He is sure we'll be happy to hear
our *patron* will be fine.
Just a case, very common, of too much black bile.
Had we noticed he'd been melancholy
of late?

Señor Ortiz has never quite been
what I'd call jolly.
Papa shrugs. "But the Pox?" Mama asks.

Nothing more than a rash on his hands,
likely brought on by not washing.

"It seems your patron has the Old Christian
distrust of water," he smiles.
Do his eyes dance
as he says it?

We merely thank him and nod.

"One more thing. I'm sure I don't need—"
His words are so calm,
but his face betrays fear.
I quite like this man.

Papa surprises me, then, with his passion.
He takes the man's hand in his own.
But the doctor looks grateful, not shocked.

"You've nothing to fear, good sir," Papa says.
"As far as we four swear and know,
you were never here."

Summons

There's pounding at the door
before the sun's up.
My heart slams its cage.

The Office can't even send
a messenger boy
without spreading fear.

Now I thank God
for my new sleeplessness.
I hear it before
anyone wakes.

The message itself
is brief enough.

My visit *was* noted.
The Inquisitors wonder
where I have been.

I stammer out something
about being ill.
I'm given a summons,
a paper as coarse as the face
of a witch.

I lay the fire.
This page will burn
before it is seen
by my parents.

But I can't ignore it.
It's for this Friday.
I've no choice but to go.

One Life

If I tell,
will I sentence
our landlord to death?
And that dancing-eyed
doctor—what would happen
to him?

I think of that line
Papa once taught me.

The man who saves one life
saves the whole world.

I wonder, then—
is the reverse
also true?

What if you *take* one—or cause it
to be taken—to save several others?

If you do this, are you
just a rung on a ladder?
A ladder that leads
to the death of the world?

Conflict

The Office and Bea
have ordered I come
on the very same day—
the very same hour!

Is that some kind of sign from above?
I can't think of that now.

I must fix this.

"I will *not,*" says Amir.
"I've washing to do. Food's much
more important than some
bossy girl."

I can't tell him the truth
about where I must go—
or why this appointment with Bea
must *not* be shrugged off.

In the course of a week,
I've come to fear her.

The light in those eyes,
the warmth of that hand,
made me trust her.

But when she implied
that my blood wasn't pure,
I quailed.
Wouldn't you?

She might not go out of her way
to denounce us.

But what will she say if her papa,
that lapdog of the Office,
asks about me when she's angry, or slighted, or
just in her frequent foul mood?

My green face for pork
would be more than enough
to arrest us all.

Now do you see
why I'm scared of her wrath?

He must go.
He must!

Gift

Now—what should I give her?
The best thing you have.
My mind goes first
to my masterpiece.
But what would a girl who can hardly read
want with a door-stopper about Hercules?

What would *she* think is the best thing I have?

I've got it. My knife
from Toledo.
It's something a knight
might give to his lady.

They say steel from Toledo
never misses its mark.
I wonder if that includes
girls with hard hearts.

Go! He pretends to forget
what I'm talking about.
My heart sinks. I don't
have the time to fight with Amir.

"What does Papa say?" he asks, haughty.
"I don't think he'd approve
of me being seen
with that girl."

My blood heats, not just
at this slagging of Bea.
What is this talk
of *Papa*?

I roar at him.
"*My* papa wants you to listen
to me!"

He makes himself taller.
(How I hate this habit of his!)
"Perhaps Papa should know
you're a spoiled, lovesick ass!"

"You're the slave of that ass, so do
what you're told!"

That stops him cold—
for a moment. But he starts up
again.

"Papa—"

"He is *not* your papa!" and
I hit him, hard,
with the back of my hand.

"I order you! Now!
Obey me.
Get out."

I throw the knife in its scabbard
down at his feet.

He hesitates, but he takes it.
Now I must hope
he won't use it on me.

The Holy Office

I'd been expecting monsters, men
like the fire-breathing dragons from
Merlin's tales.
Ready to burn me to ash
with one insincere *Buenas dias*.

But the guard who has led me
into this room is just a young man,
barely older than me.

We don't speak.
I regard him.
He's normal as stone.
No skulls are laced
into his belt.
His fingers are grimy, but don't
end in claws.

Our eyes meet,
only once.
What had I hoped for?
A smile? An offer of friendship?
Some small sympathy?

All that is there
is a flicker of joy—
that I am I,
and he has fortune enough
to be he.

Communion

It sits on the table directly between us
like bread to be shared.
My masterpiece.

But my Inquisitor
is not hungry to see
what talent I have.

He reads me instead.
I've told him I write Spanish well,
and also a few basic Arabic words.
That sparked his regard for a moment.

But he doesn't trust me.
He points at my book.
Did you know, young master,
that this *Hercules* is unlawful?
That it is now on our List
of Heretical Books?

I look astonished.
It's not pretend.

"Well," he asks,
"what should be done
with your masterpiece?"

I rise to the challenge. I've come this far.
"Why, burn it of course, Holy Father," I say.
"The Church knows best in all things, I believe."

"But all that hard work—"
He is testing. "Each page
testifies to your art."

Two can play at knowing
the right words to say.

"I hope, Reverend Father, to fill
many more pages than that
in the course of my service
to you."

Looking for Work (2)

"Is this *really* what you came for?"
The friar leans close.
I can smell the remnants
of lunch on his breath.

What choice do I have?
I say yes.

I have no love for Señor Ortiz.
But the eyes of that doctor
dance through my conscience.
And the warm way he and Papa
shook hands.

So I've said what I say
at every strange house.
A talented scribe,
sadly out of work.

I came to *them,* after all.
If I don't pretend
that a job was the reason,
the Office will never
leave us alone.

Questions (2)

I was so calm when I woke up
this morning, so determined
to ferry this plan.

Now that it's done,
my mind roils with questions.

How will I tell Mama and Papa,
and even Amir?

(Will I tell them?)

Then, in two, too-short days,
when I start, how will I bear it?

(Will I bear it?)

Priests tell of men, desperate men,
selling their souls to the devil.

Is that what I've done?

Whose words will I put
into parchment and ink—
the denouncers? Or, perhaps,
the denounced?

And which would I rather?

I'd rather be
underground.

TWO

Amir

Cordoba, Castile and Malaga, Granada

1486–87

Falcon Like a fool, I go.
Or, like a falcon.

Let me explain.

Young boys
believe falcons are noble.
They are, after all,
kept by kings.

But here's how they train such a bird.
Tie its feet to a stick.
Strap leather blinders upon its poor eyes.
When these come off,
it has forgotten the whole notion
of freedom.

Ramon has commanded I go
to his "lady" as if I were still
his little slave boy.

What he doesn't know:
Papa (I call him that at *his* bidding)
gave me my freedom
three months ago.

Yet I am sent off
like a clever pet. To make
Master's excuse to a spoiled,
shallow girl.

Break You're not supposed to speak up.

For centuries the emirs of Granada
—*Muslim* kings—kept their bitter mouths shut.

They paid for the privilege of staying
in al-Andalus, the land they once proudly
called theirs.

When the collectors came calling from up in Castile,
the proud Southern Muslims paid up.

But every such story must end
with a change.

Our break in the chain was Abu al-Hassan.
When the King's envoy came to him for the tax,
al-Hassan sent him away.

"We do have a mint here," smiled the emir.
"But the weaklings who used it
to make coins for Christians are all dead and gone.
Today our mint makes only
scimitars' blades."

Since then, war's been brewing.
The Christian army—
led by Fernando, the King—
has many new toys and is eager to play.

I bet, were I the emir,
I'd have paid peace's price.

Watch how I'll be with Ramon, in a day:
all too glad to forgive and make nice.

How? Still,
how can I go back?

It's not just Ramon.

It's also this fact:
it's better I've gone.

If I stick around,
that Señor Ortiz will never relent.

He will chase them from there
as sure as the lion
chases the stag.

The Cathedral of Santa María

I wait.

This jewel of Cordoba
wasn't always a church.

Muslims came here
from all over al-Andalus
to say Friday prayers.

As a child in Granada
I heard of it often.

They've kept its lacework of pillars and arches.
Its splendid mosaics iced in pure gold.

But they've ruined its balance,
its simple form.

The Christians have plopped a vast choir pit—
pompous wood benches, cold, tomb-gray stone—

right in the middle. To the Christians,
it's progress. But to us few Muslim faithful

who still haunt these streets, it's
a blight. Like rouge on the face

of a ten-year-old girl, glowing without it,
just as she was.

Even the Christians don't seem to respect it.
Its courtyard, where Muslims once washed

before prayers, is famous these days
for trysts between lovers.

It is said that the mosque once contained magic.

Even filled up with thousands of the faithful,
there still felt like room for ten thousand more.

It seemed to be made,
so the chroniclers say, out of shadow and light.

Now it's no more than dead marble and stone.

Lady I've been lost in these thoughts.
So I jump when I hear boots on the tile.

A clipped, low laugh.
Not the voice of a girl.

Then, she arrives.
Swoops onto the scene like a lady at court.
Willing all eyes upon her.
Can't this girl be discreet?

Once more I think, *What* does he see?
Then I recall how angry I am.
She and Ramon are made for each other, that's all.

Will she not use her head? Stand in a less glaring spot?

If a Muslim is seen
with a Christian girl of her class—and alone…

Perhaps her honor is not dear to her.
But I like my head attached to its neck.

Now she's humming, if it
could be called that. Have I really found things
too quiet these days?
The voice of this girl could scare dragons
from out of their caves.

A Little White Square

That low laugh again. I look: there.
A clutch of young men in one corner. They ooze trouble.
I don't know what they're up to.
But I don't need Hafiz to guess
they aren't here to pray.
If they see me with Bea—

But I can't wait all day!
I stride right toward her.
Why should I fear those common thugs?

She looks up at me like I'm a boil
filled with pus.
"Ramon's very sorry," I say.
"He had an engagement, and so
could not come."
She stands there, confused.
You'd think I'd just said,
"Ramon's grown three heads."

The men in the corner are quiet.
Eavesdropping, of course.
I must be polite.

"Señorita Alvarez," I begin,
"I've been asked by Ramon
to give you a gift."

"Oh, let's get it over with,"
snorts our heroine: it's hardly becoming.
And she thrusts something at me.
It's either a token wrapped
in a white handkerchief
or else the hankie itself is the gift.
These chivalrous rites are ludicrous.
With this worthless square,
a woman pledges her heart!

I am just reaching into my sack
to pull out her gift
when it happens.
For not the first time
the world as I know it
comes to an end.

Rain I brace for that shrill voice of Bea's,
expect her to shout out
at least one *help*.

What a fool.

All I hear is the thuds of their kicks
and the hard metal rain
of their blows.

Still

I'm as still as a corpse.
No good fighting back now.

Are they gone? Better wait.
But how long can I lie here?
The day's on the wane.
If I'm caught after curfew
by the wrong men,
no excuse in the world—even being
near death—will save me from jail.

All is still. I must risk it. I open one eye.

The toe of a boot hits
like cannon shot.

One of my attackers
has returned for more.

He starts to come at me again.
What happens next I can barely remember.
Even harder is it to explain.

With the one drop of strength
that remains in my arm,
I strain for my sack, lying by me on the ground.
I thrust my hand in and grab for the knife.
Pull it out. As it comes, its sheath falls,
like magic, to the ground.
I've no strength to fight, but perhaps I can keep
the knife fast in my grip.

A loud yelp of pain, as if from a dog
that's been caught by the wheels of a cart.
My attacker, in moving to grab me,
grazed his meaty paw
on the point of my knife.

He looks at me, stunned—for a moment.
Sucks a bloodied knuckle and swears.
But he comes no closer.
His fun is done for the day.

Yet, just as he turns to run off,
he sends me a message.
He looks in my eyes.
And he smiles.

Alarm

I am fading.
My legs lack the strength
to hold me upright.

But what can I do?
Raise the hue and cry?
When a citizen sounds the alarm,
all must drop what they're doing and help.

That awful smile stops me.

It seemed to say,
Rat on me if you dare.
You are a Moor, and we
are at war with your kind.
Even if people believed
I attacked you,
would they really care?

Guardian

Papa told me
of a wonderful book he'd once copied.
It had tales of the heavens
and maps of the sky.

When he had finished
inking the names,
a gilder drew lines between stars
in pure gold.

The book quoted something
a rabbi once said ("Though
it called him a monk!" Papa scoffed):

Each blade of grass
has a guardian star
which strikes it and says to it,
Grow!

My eyes scour the heavens.
Does one of those stars
look out for me now?

Tricks

Night is turning to day when I wake.
I drag myself up,
though I've nowhere to go.

No one I pass stops to offer
me help. They seem angry, in fact.

They scowl at my wounds
and they show me their backs.

Are this limp and this blood
only tricks I've invented?

Props I've designed to rob peace
from their sleep?

Manumission

I saved up my money.
Washed clothes to help them
put food on their table.
But then, without telling Mama or Papa,
I doubled my clients.

There I was in the dark hours of morning,
scrubbing cloth in the Guadalquivir.
Ramon complains he can't sleep
with me there, but the truth is,
he can, and he does—like a log.
Not once did he hear me
creep out.

Papa was shocked
when I showed him my handful of coins.
Then he retrieved a piece of parchment.
It seemed to shine brighter
than a whole chest of maravedis:
it lit up his face.

"I'd already prepared this, Amir.
I hope the Arabic is halfway correct."

I, Isidore Benveniste, hereby manumit Amir,
son of Aman Ibn Nazir of Granada.

Manumit. Every slave knows that word.
The thought of its sound often sings us to sleep.

There were more fancy lines in his beautiful script.

I was free! "I won't take your money, Amir.
In fact, had I some of my own, it is I who'd pay you.
You have taught me so much."

Mama came in.
"Amir," she said kindly,
"will you stay on as what you've become?
As our son?"

The Muslim Quarter

I'm ashamed to admit it,
but apart from my Friday
prayers at the mosque,
I've steered clear of this place.

It reminds me too much of all I have lost.
My birthplace. My home.
(And now I've lost two.)

I go deeper in than I've ventured before.
The mosque sits on the fringe of the quarter,
where the Christians can keep it under
their eye.

In the few streets behind, though, Mudejares
live by the handfuls of hundreds.

Will anyone notice one more?

Call to Prayer

No muezzin calls
from a tall minaret.

No matter.
All the men know it.
It is time for prayer.

They stream from all over.
Carpenters, masons,
even men without work.
They make for the mosque
with sure, silent steps.

Many come from outside the quarter.
It is like watching birds
converge for a flight.

I don't join them yet. Instead,
I crouch in an alley
between two slender homes.

I don't want to be seen.
I'm afraid of more blows or, worse, jail.
I fear kindness too.

I must be alone. I must think.
But it gives me a glimmer of comfort
to witness these men and their small,
frequent journey to talk
to our God.

Stir

Black night.
Nothing stirs here.
Wait—that *was* something.

Was it? Was that deepened shadow,
so fleeting, a person?
Does someone look down
from that window up there?

If I'm seen, I must go.
That Christian—the villain who beat me,
and grinned—will say *I* menaced him.
With a weapon, no less.
I know how it goes.
That is more than enough
to earn death, for a Moor.

No, there is no one.
It was only a bird.

Bird The bird
is an angel.

When I wake, I am under
a soft woolen blanket.
A bowl of clear water
is here by my head.
My brow is still damp
from the kiss of a cloth.

There is also a loaf of warm bread
and—praise Allah—a single boiled egg.

I look at the window.
I notice, in this light, that it's covered up
by a cunning black screen.
The person inside can see out—
but no one outside can see in.

Such screens are used
by young girls in books—
girls too pretty to be gazed upon.
Well, this is no time
for romantic tales.
I'm no ass like Ramon!

I must bathe my wounds
and move on.

Sanctuary

If ever I've needed to pray,
it is now.

I want to be pure for my God,
but the ablution baths
are up three large steps.
I'm too weak to climb.
Allah, I decide, will understand.
That bowl of clear water
I bathed my wounds with
will serve Him this time.

I pray, then I lie in a dark, quiet spot.
No one looks twice.
This mosque is our place, as Muslims,
to meet, and to pray, and to act
like the free men the Crown
says we are.

But it's locked at night.
There have been problems.
I've heard this before.

Some Christians can't manage
to hold their strong wine.

They come here to take out their anger
on what we hold dear.
Last year, a part of the *mihrab*—the holiest
spot in the mosque, facing Mecca—
was smashed into bits.

So at night I return
to the alley.

I know I am seen.
But I'm weak.

Each morning,
the loaf, and the egg,
and the cool, refilled bowl.

Each midday, I say
to myself: Move on.

But each evening,
I answer:
Just one night more.

Christians and Moors

This morning my bowl is knocked over,
stopping a dream of a boot
to my head.

An army has come to the quarter.
But this army is not one to fear—
except as a sign of times soon to be here.

It's merely a pageant of war—
an annual game of the Christians.
Young boys fierce as puppies skitter about.
The ones dressed as Muslims have tin scimitars
and beards scrawled on chins with burnt cork.

Of course it's the cross that carries the day.
The boys playing Christians thrust swords
at the sky, one foot on the backs of the
quick-vanquished Moors.

It's not always like that in life.
Remember the rout in the Axarquia?
We're harder to conquer
than children at play.
(Children instructed to lose!)

Last month, Ramon and I watched
as the army filed out of Cordoba,
off to fight the Muslims in the South.
There were twelve thousand men
riding on horses; behind them, on foot,
five times that.

They clearly know that their task will be hard!

Friend

This morning, the door closes just
as I turn round to look.
Missed him again.
Or, missed her.
Each night, I've tried to sit up
so I'll see who it is.
But my head and my heart
are too heavy.
I sleep.

I dream
of our Cordoban courtyard.
The soul-soothing shade
of its one lemon tree.

Mama is there.
We trade stories about
our darkest hours.
Our finest ones too.

When I wake here
on this patch of ground,
I can't recall one single thing
that we said in my dream.

But I feel refreshed.
And the cool morning air
seems to carry the scent
of a lemon tree.

Slaves There is a feast in the mosque's small courtyard.
A cluster of African Muslims are honored guests.
They were captured by pirates and brought to Castile
for quick sale—in the very slave markets
I know too well.

But the good Mudejares of Cordoba
have saved them. They have pooled
their resources to buy the men free.

The African Muslims make speeches. Their words,
to me, sound more like Chinese
than Arabic. Are their accents strange?
Or has it just been so long
since I've heard my own tongue?

I do catch some. They speak of the tactics
of Fernando's army.
The Crown's soldiers pillage and kill without mercy.
Not only that—they raze and destroy
the very land they would have for their own!
They burn fields, smash down dams.
Leave nothing alive.

I lurk. My belly, amid these fine smells, does
whirligigs.
When I think I can no longer stand it
I look at the ground.
A dish of meat stew steams by my knee.
Smells of cinnamon, garlic, and lamb.
And another scent too.

Just what a beautiful dove
of a woman would wear.

Friend (2)

This quarter has its own sheriff, a fat Mudejar
employed by the Queen.

Still, later that night, it's a Christian official
who comes to disperse us.

Muslims are breaking the law of the land
if they meet for longer than pleases the Queen.

So we go our own ways.
But when I get back

to my square of earth,
a man is there. I can see

that he's waiting for me. I stop.
He holds out his hand.

"Don't be afraid, son," he says.
"I'm a friend."
A round, perfect egg
lies there in his palm.

Free

I'm having a good laugh at myself.
Beautiful dove of a woman, indeed! It seems
I'm not so above Ramon after all—
concocting a lithe young protectress
instead of this solemn old bear of a man.

Then I see her.

Only her eyes are uncovered.
But their light shines brighter
than seven boatloads of yellow
Bea hair.

"My daughter says she has fed you,
my friend," the man says. "For a week!
You are lucky my daughter is fond
of defying the rules of her parents."

Her eyes smile.
It's too sweet to endure.
But that is not why
I must look away.

It is as if I'm a small boy again, no more
than three. And I sit at a table with my
dear mother.
Time stands still, for a breath, in its glass.

We are, both of us, in this instant, here.
And both of us free.

Free (2)

It doesn't take long—talk turns to war
and shatters the spell.

"We want only peace," this man says.
"To be left to ourselves."

"But you are not free." I shouldn't insult them.
Not when I owe them my life.
Yet, after so many days of unbroken silence,
my tongue yearns to talk.
"With all respect, sir, you belong to the Queen.
You pay extra taxes so you may exist.
This, in the place where we once
ruled as caliphs and emirs!"

The man is not angered.
He, too, wants to talk.
"You are young," he tells me,
shaking his head.

"Maybe so. But sages deem
slave years are ten times as long
as ones spent in freedom," I say.
"In those, I'm afraid, I'm old enough.
And I'm tired."

My next words are more
for myself than for him.
"I want the rest of my years
to be free."

Normal

As I walk to the mosque the next morning,
a crier stops me—stops us all—
in our tracks. What does he care
that it's time for our prayers?

A Moor, shouts the crier,
is wanted by the alcalde—the sheriff of the Queen.
He is sought for intent to murder a Christian,
and for consorting with a Christian girl.

All that is known are his age—
around seventeen—and initials, R.B.
Anyone knowing a Moor who fits
this description should report him at once
to the sheriff.

Ramon Benveniste. The sheath from his knife...
it fell, I remember. I didn't retrieve it.
It must have worn his initials.

How much of what happened did Bea see?
No matter, I think.
She failed to stop it, or even
to try—I surely can't trust
that she'd vouch for me now!

For a moment, last night,
I dreamed of a life that was normal.
A father (well, father-in-law). A tall house.
A wife.

Leave off dreaming, Amir.
It is time to go home.

Leave-taking

I look round in vain
for a pen and some ink.

But what words are there
to explain everything?

It's too soon. We've only
just met. It would be saying hello
and good-bye in one breath.

I search in my satchel
for something to give.
I can't leave the knife. It might
bring them trouble.

Then—what's this?
A white linen square—Bea's gift.
I've not yet looked inside.

I look now.
Nestled in there
is a tiny white tooth.
On one of its sides
is a nasty brown hole
in the shape of a heart.

I can't leave this!

Perhaps I'll drop it
in some pit I pass,
or the Guadalquivir.
The sooner the better.
The tooth seems to bite through my satchel,
saying, "Watch out, Amir!"

The Return

It seemed likely I'd find
a new boy—a new slave—
asleep in my bed. No, Amir,
don't be bitter. You must never forget
Papa's kindness to you.

Second father, I know.
But no less true for that fact.
How can I leave him?
I can't, my heart says.
Yet how can I stay? Though I am
a free man, Ramon can't grasp it.
Nor can the rest of Castile.

I wait long at our door, listening.

At first, I hear nothing.
Then, finally—there.
The snotty, moist rattle I'd know anywhere.
Ramon sleeps.

And it's there, by my pillow, just as before.
Tell me, Hafiz, what should I do?

Come, for our hopes are no more than a broken-down house.
Bring wine. Life's foundations are rooted in wind.

Well, there's no wine around
and no money to buy it.
But I know I'll take you.

A Broken Mouthful

I think of leaving
the knife for Ramon.
But after what's happened,
it feels like a curse.
I don't truly wish
any evil on him.

And, once again,
I play with the thought
of a note. I hate to imagine what
Mama and Papa are thinking.
That I've hated it here, so I've run away.
That I've found them cruel.
That I didn't believe
they loved me like a son.

There's not enough ink
in Castile to convey
the armies of thoughts
that clash in my brain.

I would like to make peace
with Ramon.
But there are times
when peace just becomes
a broken mouthful.
A word that no tongue in the world
can pronounce.

Whip I head South.

My only companion, the sun.
By mid-morning, it's no longer welcome.

I have always loved its kiss on my back.
But today it's the bite of a whip that won't quit.

I daydream of water.
When the caliphs ruled here in al-Andalus
they tapped rivers' gifts the way Orpheus
could draw songs from a reed.
Wells and fountains bordered every path.

The Christians believe that bathing
too much is immoral. What's more,
so they say, it makes a man lesser.
Weakened in combat, unlikely to win.

What a stink those battlefields will be!
I almost laugh as I think it.

My mirth is short-lived.
A young wraith on a sweating horse
comes charging at me from out of nowhere.

He yanks the cantina from my sagging neck.
Its buckle catches the cloth on my head;
he wrenches it free and is gone.

That vessel was empty. The joke is on him.
But what will I fill when I find the next stream?

If ever I do?

Shades of Brown

I am walking so weary
I can't lift my head.

I play at analogies,
as I often did with Papa.
He loved to compare
two different things, to find
their shared ground.

So: a likeness for each separate shade—
there are many—of brown.

There's the brown of my feet peeking out
from their sandals, as brown, you might say,
as two sun-baked bricks.

There's the brown of a grouse in the thicket
just there, lighter, like oven-warmed bread.

And then there's the heartbreaking brown
of a bare riverbed, rusty red like dried blood.

There's the golden-hued brown of these endless
wheat fields
—a sunset, maybe, that has fallen to Earth.

There is—
I just about trip
right over the men.

A roar of laughter goes up, a lion of mirth.
They must have been watching me walk
for an age.

"What's the matter, young thinker?
Have we not enough gear to merit your gaze?"

What parched breath I have
dies quick in my throat.
I have never seen so much steel in one place.
Five—no, six—cartfuls of weapons.
Crossbows and maces and long, glinting swords.
Behind those, two pipes much the size of large bears,
things I've seen only in pictures, in books.
But I know full well what they are.
They spit fire.

Numbers This whole grisly stockpile for a handful of men?
What kind of army is this?
Or do their companions
lie crouched in ambush, expecting
a thousand more versions of me
to stumble among them?

I brace myself, ready to flee.
Nothing happens. I'm exhausted.
The men see it, laugh once again.

"Go ahead—run. We won't chase you!" says one.
"But how about something to eat?
You look like a twig that's ready to snap."

Ours

The men explain it: they're Jews.
From Toledo, where Jews, years ago,
were not all expelled.

"Anyway, there remain many Jews in al-Andalus,"
one tells me. He frowns. "Why shouldn't there be?
We've been here since the Romans.
A thousand long years."

I grope for my voice. "I don't wish to fight, friend.
We're all of us worthy wanderers here."

He nods. My answer was good.
"We're off to the city of Malaga.
The King is conducting a siege
on the Muslims who rule it.
It is we, Jews of the realm, who must
carry the arms."

Will they fight?
They will not. They support neither side.
Then they're free? (I must ask.)
"As free," says this man, "as can be
when a King and a Queen call you *ours*."

The Captive

"Enough questions for us, little thinker. You're the mystery here.
Let me see. Escaped slave? Your master's a prick?
You slept with the lady of the house?
Or the daughter? Or both?"

I smile. I'm too weak for banter.
But my eyes are drawn
to a man in their midst.
He's chained to the wheel
of a cart by the ankle.

"Oh, him?
He's a Christian. You'd think him
fortunate, yes? And yet
he's an unfortunate Christian indeed.
He's wanted by *them*. The Inquisition.
So we've been asked to bring him along.
Can you guess what he's done?"

I can't begin to, but that
does not seem to be called for.
He goes on, barely stopping
for breath.

"He tried, the poor man, to convert to *our* faith.
Strange, in these times, is it not?
But he said that the Church, which roasts
men like meat, is no place for him.
So he went to a synagogue in Toledo
and asked for instruction.
The rabbi he talked to was no braver
than we who carry these arms.
Fearing for his life, he reported our friend
to the Office.

"Now it is Jews who must jail him,
adding stranger to strange.
We daren't say no.
And besides, what other work
is there left for Jews in this land?

"But he's just passing through us.
A ghost passing through
a wall of more ghosts.

"Though fit enough food
for the Holiest fires."

Pockets

I'm astonished.
They bother with *autos-da-fé*
in the midst of their war?

"Of course! And why not?
The Queen sees the stake and the sword
as tools with one purpose—
a pure Christian Spain.
And the King says the Inquisition is fire—
if you'll pardon the expression—
for his men's morale."

"Not to mention the means
to buy all these toys!" A man
with a button-round nose has piped up.
"No one's buried with full pockets, my friend!
As long as backsliders are burned at the stake,
there'll be money to grease the costly machine
of this war with the Moors."

My head reels.
It all seems an endless circle.

I recall Ramon's words.
This bloodthirsty place.

At this rate, we'll all have to wait
till we die to escape it.

Trade

The captive won't tear his gaze
from the ground.
I can't seem
to stop staring at him.

His clothes are those of any Christian.
He wears no *sanbenito*. Not yet.
"Trade up," the men urge me.
They eye my red Mudejar badge, my turban,
my ankle-length robes.
"You can't pass the armies
of the King wearing those!"

"Aren't you forgetting," I ask them,
"one little thing? Shall I say
my dark skin is a sunburn?"

The men laugh.
"There is many a Christianized Moor on the side
of the King.
They are prized, in plain fact.
They can talk to the traitors who sneak
from inside to sell news of the city.
Though no one's suggesting that you
would do *that*."

Still, I refuse. How much worse for this
man if he's seen in my clothes.
A Judaizing Christian in Mudejar robes!

That night, there's a party.
The men drink sweet Juarez wine
from the cask.

The wretch runs. I see him, and pretend
I'm asleep. But he trips. Someone wakes.
An arrow pierces his back
before he can get to his feet.

"*Now* will you take his clothes?"

Allah forgive me.
Yes.

Gift

It's the last thing I do
with his body.
I've already dressed him
in my turban and robe.

But before I depart
I give one final gift.

Bea's square of white linen
—and her little tooth.

I feel sorry for leaving
this legacy.

I just want it gone.

Praying

After two weeks of wheat fields,
they've finally vanished!
Lush vineyards spice the moist air.
Olive trees speckle
the rolling green hills.

These are the banks
of the River Xenil.
We're making progress:
the Axarquian Mountains
spike the distance.

As much as we can,
we camp near a stream.
These have extra value for me,
for my prayers.
I plunge hands and feet
in the cool water.
At last, I am clean for my God.

I bring my sack with me, the money I earned.
Some of the men in our party
have little to lose.

But one day while praying
I pay for my doubts.

I turn round as a bandit—not one of the Jews—
streaks off.

With him, my satchel.
All I have in the world.

Not So

I still have Hafiz!

He is inside the blanket I use as a pillow,
just where I stowed him last night.

His worn cover mocks me.

This is the sum of your worldly goods now!

I open the pages.
Here's what he says:

The lily and rose always rise once again
in the spring, but to what purpose?
Nothing is permanent.

Including Ramon's knife—my sole weapon—
and the few coins I'd saved, so it seems.
Much help you are, only friend.

Blank Pages

On the sixth day each week, we stop.
Jews must not work on their Sabbath.
And they certainly can't
carry cartloads of weapons!

"What if those bandits come back on your Sabbath?"
I ask them.
"May you defend yourselves if attacked?"

This starts a debate that lasts through the night.
I soon give up trying to follow its turns.
I dig out the quill from my new leather satchel.
Both are gifts from the Jews, who pitied my loss.

I open Hafiz.
There are pages left blank at the back of the book.
Perhaps, Allah willing, I'll write.

Rooster Allah, there's so much that's odd going on in your world.

If I could get you to come for a talk,
it would be a long one.

But I'd have to start somewhere.
So here's what is on my mind now.

Why are the nights so terribly long?

The men say it's foolish to travel in darkness.
We're too easy prey for the bandits who hide
in the mountains nearby.
So we camp, and we sleep. Or we try.

Though the days now grow longer with summer's advent
the nights, too, seem to stretch.
The men grow bored, and then restless.
They drink and they fight.

I also do battle,
but my jousts are with words.
The men call me "rooster" for my scratching quill.

Nothing I try turns out right.
The book's few blank pages are taking a beating.
The parchment is thin as gossamer now
from the scraping and changing I've done.

In all these cartloads of equipment, not one pumice stone!
I've only the rocks that I find on the ground
with which to erase.
They're no match for my scores of misrhymes
and mistakes.

Hafiz, there's one thing, in all your complaints,
you've forgotten to say.

Poetry is hard!

Friend (3)

Sol—the button-nosed one—
must want to be friends.

He shows me a sketch of his wife—it's quite good.
He boasts of his sons. He has sons?
He doesn't seem all that much older than me.

Sol asks no questions, but it's more than clear.
He hopes that I'll crack.
A pomegranate, withholding my seeds.
All that it takes is the tap of the spoon
on the skin.

I'm touched by his kindness.
But I don't open up.

I've lost the talent for friendship, I think.
And maybe the taste.

Friend (4)

One time we played
a great game of tag,
just like boys half our age.

Ramon and I ran and we ran
through our quarter.
Down blind alleys and skinny lanes.
Across every bridge that we saw.
We wound up in places we'd only heard of—
and some that we hadn't.

Cordoba's streets wind and turn
like knots in the hair of Medusa.
It was fun.

Ramon won.
(I half let him, knowing his pride.
Nothing is too small
to irk it.)

"That, my friend,
was an excellent game,"
Ramon said.

My friend.

Is such a word real
when one man is free
and the other is not?

Chains Some of these Jews
can read very well.
A few, even bits
of Arabic. Under the caliphs,
Jews spoke that language
nearly as well as the Muslims.
Words here and there were passed on.

One of these men asks to borrow Hafiz.
I'm ashamed at how loath to share him I am.
For help, I remember
how quick Papa was to loan out his books.

The first man who bought me, Señor Barico,
was decent enough. He neither flogged me
nor kept my legs chained. Not like some.

But he did chain his books.
He must have owned hundreds.
I never touched one.
He slept with his favorites
as though they were pillows.

Señor Barico struck me only once.
I had set down his cup
too close to a book.

"Dimwit!" he boomed.
"Never put water where it could be spilled
and run the ink!"

After, he was sorry.
"I know you can't love
books as I do."

Señor didn't know
that his slave could read.
Slaves don't correct masters.

He never found out
how wrong he was.

Mountains After more than a fortnight of walking
the real labor starts.

The mountains are no longer distant.
Once we desired just to reach them.
Now we are in them, and
all tangled up in their tricks.

It's a contest between the wagons and men—
which moan the most going up the steep slopes?

Sol laughs at us.
"Imagine," he says, "how you'd have fared
six months ago! I was here, so I know.

"These roads we walk on? Not there.
Since that time, six thousand men
have been paving the way for your
precious feet!"

Well, even with bridges and roads,
it's hard work. The curves are sharp elbows.
It's easy to slip. The spring rains were heavy,
and there have been floods.
My clothes have become so caked with mud,
they weigh at least twice what they did
when I took them (I shudder)
from the Christian's corpse.

And yet, for the first time in weeks,
I feel awake.
Perhaps work revives me.
Or maybe it's just that these mountains
are filled with my *abba*—my father.
My first.

Mountains (2)

He'd leave us to climb them, stay away long,
and then, happy day, he'd return.
His cart when he came would be brimming with snow,
packed in as tight as skin stretched on a drum.

He always came down to a crowd.
The best men in Granada waiting for him.
The courtiers—even the emir himself—
bought up each flake of snow every time.
Some had fancy wives who bathed in it,
swearing it made them as young as their daughters.
Some topped it with raisins, ate it like candy.
Most used it to give longer life to their food.

But no matter which grandees clamored around,
my *abba* would wait. He refused to remove
one bit of snow till he saw that I'd come.

As people queued up for his wares,
he'd conjure the finest snow cone—all for me.

Pure and plain was how I preferred it.
Nothing to muddy the clean, bracing flavor,
exactly the same as the mountain air's taste
when sometimes it breezed by my bed.

Only once in Cordoba did I taste that air.
I was out on the patio, watching the stars.
The air changed, just for a minute, and there
was the smell of the mountains.

It was as if my first father, and I, had not left.

Why Not?

Those long days of waiting
for *abba*'s descent,
my mother and I learned to read
side by side.

So many times had I stared at those scribbles,
wondering how men saw stories in them.
In Granada, writing is part of the world.
It's not just in books. It graces the walls
of our homes and our mosques.
It is the way we talk to our God.

Mother did washing for a poor scholar.
In exchange, he gave us one lesson each week.
These were just threads.
But we used them to make
a whole carpet. Learning one word
always leads to another.

So when Raquel—my Cordoban mama—
said, "Women don't read," I asked her,
"Why not?" And she had no answer.

Papa and Ramon echoed her, though.
"Women don't read." (Or had she echoed them?)
Females have poor heads for books,
so they said. I knew better.

So during siestas when Papa was tired,
too tired for work on our project together,
Mama and I worked instead.

We'd sit in the courtyard with what books
we could find. Even *Plants of Castile*.
I knew some Spanish, but not enough.
She helped with meanings.
Though sometimes we simply listened
to the music of words.

We were, in that courtyard, shut off from the world.
But also, somehow, more in it than ever.
Gathering threads.

Ghosts

One day my *abba* went up the mountain
and did not come back down.
Three snowfalls came and three snowfalls went.
His cart, even then, was not to be seen.
After four snows, a new man appeared.
He had a new cart.
And no word of my father.
So he said.

The city forgot all about my *abba*.
He'd never been.
The townsfolk began to ignore us—
my mother and me.
We were cursed, and maybe contagious.

We became walking ghosts
without friends.
Perfect food for the slave-making pirates
who came from the coast, searching out weakness.
Harvesting ghosts.

Not Me

That was the last
that I saw of my mother.
Two men
dragged her one way.
Two more
dragged me another.

Faces in windows disappeared quickly.
People talking
across narrow lanes
instantly hushed and withdrew.
All gone in an eyeblink,
as if we had dreamed them.

And we were alone in the world.

Now that I'm older
I understand better.
Those faces were hiding.
Those people, each saying the very same prayer.
It exists in all tongues, no matter what version
of God you believe.

It goes something like this:
Please, God—not me.

Malaga Just before we were
(I really don't know what word
I can use)
taken,
my mother and I hatched a plan.

She'd been born in Malaga.
She had two brothers—might they still be there?
She worried these brothers might not believe
my *abba* had disappeared.
Men don't just vanish!
They might suspect that she'd run away.
Deserted her husband.
Bringing them shame.

Or, they'd believe her.

"Should we take the chance?"

I said yes.

"After all," I told her,
"we have nothing to lose."

Never say that.

As long as there's freedom,
there is something to lose.

Slave Market, Cordoba

When Señor Barico took me to his home
and then unfastened my heavy leg chains,
I could hardly believe what he'd done.

I paced in my room the whole of that night.
I kept up till I dropped.

I feared if I let my legs rest for one minute,
someone would enter and chain them again.

The Sea

A change in the wind
brings the salt tang of sea.

Ramon often spoke
of this moment.
What it would be like
the first time you sensed it.
Smelled it or heard it, or even
just felt its wet breath
on your skin.
And then, when it came
into view—!

Ramon talked, and I
gazed at the ground.
I didn't tell him the sea
called me too.

But I feel no elation
now that I approach.
My heart is full of foreboding.

Of all the places I've wandered, all the people
I've been, war is the last place for me.
When we do reach the sea
maybe I'll dive in.
Though I don't even
know if I know
how to swim.

Home

I once harbored dreams
of triumphant return.

I would stand at the gates of Granada, my Kingdom,
no longer a slave. Through my exploits,
I would have become a great Muslim prince!

All things—crowds of my subjects,
gates of stone and steel—
would part graciously as I passed.
"Amir's an emir!" the people would cry.
Instead, here I am.
Dressed like the enemy.
No scimitar, nor even
a flat Christian sword
in my hand.

A stranger,
a zero,
in my own land.

New City

Outside the tall walls of Malaga,
a whole city of Christians has bloomed
from the ground.

Thousands of tents of all colors;
horses decked out in crimson and gold.

Stealth, it is clear, is not this camp's game.
A carpet of tulips would draw less notice.

Banners flap in the wind.
Soldiers from all ends of Europe
polish their armor with spit as they sing.

One of the tents is as large as the ships
plying the harbor at our backs.
Its flag tells the tale:
it houses the King.

There are bakers and blacksmiths
and artists with easels, drawing the scene.
No one wants to miss out.
Malaga and then, at long last, the capital city,
Granada itself.
The finishing strokes of a great masterpiece.
The title?
The Holy Reconquest of Spain.

Large groups of traders sit cooling their heels.
If the wall should come down, the plunder will start.

Men playing cards. Men having jousts. A few women
too, lending themselves for a price. The priests—
of course, there are many of these—dog their steps.

"Men, don't succumb to the devil!" they warn.
"Beware! Repent! Shun these women and pray!
Like the Moors' fortress, you are under siege!
The forces of evil will seep through the cracks
of even the stoutest armor."

Siege

It's a strange kind of warfare:
a battle of waiting.

The kitchen tents snuggle as close
to the wall as is safe.

Too close and Malaga's women, defiant and fierce,
will stand on the ramparts, pouring
boiling oil down upon
the cooks' heads.

Close enough to be sure
the aroma of meat—today, roasting lamb—
rises over the wall.
So it may attack
the besieged where they starve.

Leave-taking (2)

Sol and the others have left for Seville.
It's hard to believe there's a need for more weapons,
but those are their orders.

I'm surprised how I feel as they leave.
When will I learn I'm alone in this world?

I'm weary of this waking sleep
of not doing.
I must find a way
to get through that wall.
I won't find my uncles
in this carnival!

But—short of becoming an arrow—
how will I do it?

Line Still the carts keep on coming.
Mound after mound of weapons and food.
No wonder taxes are high in Castile!
I think of what Sol said when we met.
New Christians, should they place even
one toe astray, are burned for the money this takes.

I fear for Papa, and Mama, and even Ramon.
They are conversos, and have done one thing, at least,
too close to the line.
That book of Papa's, the one that tells of
his ancestor's life. I helped with it.

His great-grandfather once worked on a Talmud—
a holy Jewish book.
Papa included quotations from it
in that book of his own.

In the law of the Christians,
that is heresy.
Would it be enough
to send them to the stake?
It's such a small thing.
But I bet it would.

Now I can't eat the meat
these Christians serve.
The smell of it roasting conjures
the flesh that has bought it.

Talk There are perils this side of the wall besides hunger.
After living like ants for nearly three months,
men begin to take ill. Rumors of poxes and plagues
have blossomed,
though no one is saying in which tents they live.

Men bored beyond reason pick fights in the night.
They race dogs and bait bears.
One of these last breaks free from its torments.
It mauls several men.

How much longer, they shout, can these Moors
hold out?
What are they eating, their fingers and toes?
Talk of dark magic spreads through the camp.
The Malagans have struck up a deal with the devil!
They can go without food in this life—
And he'll eat their souls when they're dead.

Call to Prayer (2)

One thing I know about the Malagans:
they still pray.

The sweet, sorrowful voice of the muezzin
calls the people to prayer
five times each day.
It spirits over the ramparts.
It can't be contained.

The first time I hear it I know
what it is. It sounds like the cry
of a ghost to its love.
It sounds like the voice of Allah himself.

For those moments, I travel.
I'm once more a child.
I am through the walls.

The Queen's Arrival

Just when the boredom is set to ignite,
Isabella arrives like a saint in the flesh.

Even crusading soldiers from foreign lands
lower their flags in salute as she passes.
The King and his men ride in full state toward her.
Two mountains, it seems, have agreed to unmoor
and to meet.

And what finery! Her Majesty's mule
(he's a rich chestnut brown)
has a saddle of silver and gold.
The beast is more like a throne than an ass.

The soldiers are moved.
Their backs look much straighter.
For the first time in weeks, their eyes seem to shine
without mischief.

The first thing the Queen does:
lead the men in a prayer.
Say what you will about Isabella.
She believes in her God.

Doghouse

Restless, I haunt the edges of camp
like one of the dogs.

I've added it up and I'm shocked.
I've been in this camp for nearly a month!

Part of me says,
Make a break for it.

You don't belong on this side.
You *must* cross.

But if I were seen, it would scarcely matter
who'd found me. Each side would think me

a traitor or spy. They would battle to see
who could fill me with arrows the fastest!

Trade (2)

Some Malagans emerge from the city,
arms stretched out before them
like sleepwalkers.

I might count each of the bones in their chests
if I could stand to keep looking.

They've come to surrender. They must eat.

They're made to wait in one ragged line,
as if this trade were normal.

But I know what it is.

For now, one grudging handful of bread.
Forever, the life—the not-life—
of a slave.

Invasion A clutch of Muslims from nearby Guadix
have come to help the Malagans.
They bring satchels of food
and a few extra weapons.
But first they must break
through the Christian lines.

Only a few are successful. They throw themselves into
the poor, starving city. Good luck to them!
They are brave men, if not very smart.

Most are captured before they get in.
Soldiers cut them to pieces without wasting time.
One begs for his life. His words are a gallop.
He speaks Arabic. He clasps forth his gaunt, shaking
hands.
Does he beg for conversion?
The Queen has forbidden men to be killed
with their hands in the posture of Christian prayer.

They need a translator.
I make myself small, try to shrink deep as I can
in the crowd.

I am seen.
A guard calls me over.

It seems I have not
been the ghost that I thought.

A Knight?

I'm afraid, once they see
the *S* on my face,
they'll ask questions for which
no answer will save me.

But her Majesty's man gets
straight to the point.

"What is it, señor, that this man is saying?"

I listen closely once more,
though I heard well enough.

"He wishes to see Their Highnesses.
In private. He says that he *must*.
He has key information, he says, that will help you—
that is, us—in this war."
I translate with ease.
Isabella's man thanks me and says, "You may go."

I don't know what I expected.
That he'd lay his broad sword on my shoulder
and knight me right there?

Well, maybe.
Still, I'm not disappointed.
Rather, I must chide myself
for feeling apart and—I'll admit it—
aglow.

Miracle The story is legend as soon as it happens.
I'll try to recount it as best I can.

The man is brought to the tent
of the King and Queen.
But Fernando is napping. Even in wartime,
his *siesta*'s supreme. Isabella defers
till her husband should wake.

The Muslim is put in a neighboring tent
while everyone waits. Unknown to the guards,
a lady is there with the Portuguese prince.
Who's to say what they're doing?
The Moor comes across them.
He understands nothing they say.
But he sees their rich clothing. He believes
they're the monarchs. Those whom he seeks.

He pulls from his mantle a dagger
and stabs the young prince in the head.
Next, he goes for the lady.
But her screams bring the guards
and their swords. He is quickly dead.

When the Queen hears of this
too-close brush with her end
she falls to her knees.
A miracle is declared.
God saves the lives
of his rulers on Earth yet again.

In this way the Queen
tells herself that her deeds
please God's eyes.
Even those, like the *autos-da-fé,* that are so pitiless
hardened men look away.

Commerce

Miracle or no, the treacherous try
sours the mood in the camp.
The King's catapult, a dragon of wood,
volleys the corpse of the trickster
right over the wall.
It showers fresh blood as it goes.

The Malagans are quick
to return the grim gift.
A prisoner from inside—a Christian—
is sent out on a mule. His throat has been cut.
He hangs like a flower long dead
from the beast's back.

I thought, as a slave,
I knew how it felt
to be traded about
like a slab of cold meat.

But clearly some commerce
is worse.

I must make myself scarce.
What if they think I
was part of that trick?

What, though, is my life really worth? Even to me?
My fear tells the truth:
it's worth something.

And my heart hammers this:
I might want to live.

Gunpowder

It was Muslims, they say,
who first brought it to al-Andalus.

This is how they are thanked.

An explosion is sprung near a tower.
A key to their stronghold is breached.

Such is the wisdom
of murderous gifts.

Hail the Moor-slayer

The men in the camp rally so suddenly
you'd think they'd been stalled there
a day, not three months.

Raised on the ramparts, the proud ensign
of Santiago. Saint Iago, renowned slayer of Moors.
Ramon has a doll in his form.

A voice cries, "By Santiago!"
"Santiago!" the men in the camp answer as one.

The name vibrates through me
as though I myself have shouted it out.

Terms

The wait is not over.
Delegations come out
from the vanquished city
to talk out the terms of surrender.

None of us knows what is said.
But each time the Malagans emerge
from the royal tent, their faces have lengthened.
They look afraid.

Three times they come.
Three times they go back.

I suppose they're among the city's elite.
But their clothes hang like rags.

Are my uncles, as merchants of silk,
among these brave men?

I must find my moment.
But daren't approach.

No matter.
The moment finds me.

No A voice barks, "You there."
I don't move. "You there! Boy!"

Why do I know it means me?

I should ignore it.
But, like a falcon,
I'm trained all too well.

I look up.

"You are that translator, no?"
It's the Queen's man.
"Come, ride with me.
Our sovereigns can use you."

And the man sweeps me onto
the back of his horse before
I can agree with him:
No.

Sight

I wish I didn't have eyes,
to see such things.

Bodies—my people—litter the streets.
And animals, dead and rotting, everywhere.

I pass by a horse with its side torn for food.
A woman lies sobbing, crunched in a heap.
When I approach her, she jolts to her feet.
Flees like she thinks I'll cut off her head.

And the sound. It's strange, a high hum,
as from a guitar with only one string.
But it's nothing like music.
I can't stop my eyes.
They look to the bodies.
The sound's made by flies.

To think I once cringed at the thought
of soldiers—alive ones—
who don't favor baths.

The Fortress of Gibralfaro

A much different sound from the hilltop,
last holdout of the Malagan Moors.
Huzzah!
The fortress itself has surrendered.
The crescent-moon banner is torn from the ramparts
and impaled on the blade of a sword.

In its place goes a flag with the sign of the cross.
I hear strains of the Christian *Te Deum,*
their triumphal hymn.

My rider dismounts and he kneels at the sight.
I kneel too—for a minute:
then use the chance of bowed heads
as the wings for my flight.

Doors

Heralds move through the city,
proclaiming.
Malaga is now
a part of Castile.

They charge everyone
to stay in their houses.

By the good offices
of the merciful Queen,
food and drink will be brought
to the door of each family.

Stray from your homes,
and you'll miss your chance.

And what of us vagabonds
without even a door?

The Torment of Bells

It's true once again—
the Queen trails decorum behind her
the way ships leave a wake
in the water.

All kneel as she passes.
Her long, fur-trimmed mantle
drags Allah knows what
through the still-gory streets.

The monarchs make speeches
from the high balconies
of the alcazaba.

The Queen's theme is constant:
the war is but one more great hymn
to the glory of God.
Her confessor, the Friar Torquemada,
sits at her side like a purring cat.
He is now Chief Inquisitor—
and the most pitiless man,
many say, in the land.
Small wonder blood flows like water
when the Queen has advisers like that!

King Fernando is much more concerned with the
present.
His attention is turned to "God's foes."
Some of the conquered Muslims
have accepted baptism. They've become "Moriscos."
But more resist it.

The King calls for all minarets—the towers of
mosques—
to be turned into belfries. The cry
of the muezzin shall be replaced with bells.

"Let the sounds of their ringing be torment,"
he shouts,
"to those infidels who refuse to take Christ.
Let the bells peal through Malaga the rest of its days."

Bells I think how Ramon would smirk at this speech.
At last, his equation of torture and church bells
confirmed!
And by no less a source than our King himself.

Mercy

The Christians are famous for mercy, you know.
Their prophet, like ours, preached about that.

But I see few signs of mercy so far.

Never mind the words of Fernando,
ringing, along with the bells, in my ears.
Infidels. Torment.
Compared to their actions,
those words are a kiss.

One bright day, a Christian, a traitor,
is killed in the plaza.
Men take turns poking him
with long, steel tipped sticks,
much the way picadors torture bulls in the ring.

They keep on with it even after he dies.
But you'd be surprised.
Death sometimes takes
a very long time.

The Cabbage

I walk through what's left of Malaga, seeking my uncles.
I'm losing all hope. The few people
I meet who will talk to me
have not heard of them. And they look at me
as if I am mad. Why search for life
amidst so much death?

When business dried up in our Cordoba shop,
food was all we could think of.
I once wrote *pastry* when I meant to write *paltry*,
marring a till-then clean page of script.

During that time I brought home a cabbage.
It was given to me by a woman whose stall
in the market we'd shopped at—when we could shop.
On this day, I offered some lines
of a poem as a trade.

"All right," said the woman, "but put me in your verse."
So I wrote a few lines in praise of Consuela, and her beauty
(not true), and prayed that the cabbage would prove
to be worth it.

(That, by the way, was my first go at a poem!
No wonder I find them so hard. Perhaps
I've been cursed by the muse for that use!)

The outside of the cabbage was wilted—nothing new there.
But each leaf, pulled back, uncovered more rot.
I peeled it in private, not wanting the others
to see how I'd failed.
Its center was black with decay.

So goes today's journey. I keep expecting
the horror to end, but it won't.
No matter how deep in the city
I go, the alleys all stink with dead things.

I push to the outskirts.
Night is falling.
At last I find a cave in a hill.
Just as I'm falling asleep
light shines in my eye.
Discovered, so soon?
Am I ready to die?

Hunger

What I see is the smallest of hands.
It barely fits round the butt of the torch.

I lift up my gaze.
A girl, no older than six, peers into my face.

When our eyes meet, she smiles.
She speaks Arabic! But not the sort that belongs
to books and discussions. This Arabic is
the sound of the streets, and the shops,
and the caves. The sound of my mother.
She speaks it so matter-of-factly I almost believe,
for a moment, I have heard
no other tongue in my life.

"Good evening, my brother.
Have you brought us some food?"

I sit up. Now I see, in the dim light of the flame,
what I hadn't before.
A whole family is here, huddled and mute,
more like some jag of rock in the cave
than people. They're that silent and still.

And their faces—
so shrunken with hunger
their eyes dwarf their cheeks.

I open my bag. In the morning I stowed there
my ration of food, as has been my practice in camp.
One never knows what the day ahead holds.

I tear it in five. Such pure joy from crumbs!
The children are grinning so wide
I can very near watch as each measly morsel
tumbles down their throats.

The youngest keeps chewing even when nothing
is left in his mouth but a few budding teeth.

The Next Morning

The children beam at me,
clearly expecting more magical food.
I cast down my eyes.
Feel like the rotten core of that cabbage
as I shuffle my way from their lives.

A man near the docks pulls pages from books.
He tears these to strips. He will boil them in water,
he tells me, until they have softened to rags.
He can wear them that way. The nights are cold here.

A sign on his cart reads, "Books and Letters."
It's in Arabic.
I take a breath, then offer
myself as a scribe.

He laughs in my face.
"Do you have nothing else but your skinny self?"

My heart flops.
I tell him.

"A book!" he scoffs. "You can see what use
I've for *those* things right now.
In Arabic too, I'll just bet.
Tell me, young clown, who in this place would
buy it from me? Have you no sword
made of feathers you'd like to sell me instead?
That would be more practical!"

But I show him which book. He actually gasps.
For one fleeting moment his eye's candle's not out.
Now he's eager to lose me.
"Take it," he says. Shoves a single maravedi in my hand.
"Good fortune to you finding something to buy."

The Cup You Hold

Of course I opened Hafiz one last time.
One line to divine the whole rest of my life.

Do I really believe in such nonsense?
Of course not.
Of course.

Here's what he said:

Respect the cup you hold. The clay it's made from
was the skulls of buried kings.

I liked that. It made sense, especially
for thinking of the past.

But what did it tell of my future?
I'll admit it. I cheated.
I opened the book once again.
How can you blame me? I was giving him up.

But Hafiz had the last laugh.

Don't be surprised at Fortune's twists and turns.
That wheel has spun a thousand times before.

If I ever have a home of my own,
perhaps I'll nail that to my door.

Cattle Call

Seven days since the capture.
Finally, the call comes.
All must repair to the great courtyard
of the alcazaba. Ten thousand Malagans—
children among them—swarm to the castle.

Soldiers preside from the ramparts.
We are framed on all sides.

Stubborn hope in the courtyard.
For hundreds of years
Muslims, Christians, and Jews
have shared the peninsula
upon which Spain rests.
What's more, this new jewel of Castile
needs people to fill it. If we promise
to live like good subjects, what should we fear?

The woman beside me is not so convinced.
Might they not just be stockpiling
fuel for their fires?

Gifts

We are, every one, to be slaves.
The Malagans have earned, says the King,
this dreadful sentence
with their stubborn hearts.

What some call stubborn,
others call brave.
This is their home, after all!
Or, it was.

One-third of the captives,
the luckiest, will go to Africa.
In exchange, Christian slaves
will be freed and returned.

Another third will be kept by the Crown.
This is payment, you see, for the high cost of war.

The remainder will go to the crusaders.
Each noble soldier who mounted this siege
will get one as a gift.

I look at the footmen who stand
on the walls. Noble?
I wonder.
They laugh at our gaunt,
stricken faces.

What kind of master
will I serve this time round?

Only Money!

Even cramped like cattle
into this square, many of us
still perform prayers.
Have they now been answered?

Fernando has given
a dribble of hope.
If the Malagans can raise—as a group—
half a million maravedis,
they may buy back their freedom.

We're given nine months.

Every man, woman, and child
must give to the Crown
a full accounting of all that they own.
Then the Crown will inform us
if it is enough.

No one sleeps.
One man stands on the shoulders
of a friend to be heard.

Rich and poor—we shall pool
our resources. How can our goods
be divided when our fates are one?

The Calculations of Clerks

There's a problem.
The clerks who make the accounts
are all Christian men, in the employ
of the Crown.

They examine our lists
with furrowed brows, like parents
assessing poor work done by children.

Some even wrinkle their noses
inspecting the treasures we have on us now.

I offer my quill.
Pretending to think, the clerk names a sum
far below its value.

It's not only quills they don't prize.
Fine lace and rich silk, even houses and orchards:
all are matched with figures so laughably low
the Malagans must struggle to hold in their anger
and not slap their smug faces.

I look at this sneering young man
who holds his own quill.
He calmly writes down the worth of our lives.
Think of *my* life a short season ago:
transcribing letters and books
for much better men.

My fingers were stained with ink spots
instead of the filth of not having washed
properly in a month.
How can that Amir and this one
be the same soul?

The Nasrid Emir

Not even close, says the head treasurer.
We have not made the sum.
People wail, wring their hands.
So much loss. And now this.

There is one hope.

Granada itself
is still Muslim.

It is said that Boabdil, the emir,
is so rich he wears ten
rings of gold on his toes.

We've just heard of some Malagan Jews
whose freedom was bought by a man from Castile.

When Boabdil hears *that,*
his pride will be stirred.
He'll saddle his Arabian horse
and bring us the money himself!

Appeals

Three messengers have gone
to Granada.

The first two came back with a promise.
We would be helped.
We must only hold on.

The third, once a long week had passed,
came back with a *no*.

The fourth
did not come back
at all.

Manumission (2)

I have an idea.
Could Papa's paper—the one that declares
I am free—
be my salvation?

If I'm enslaved again now,
I could wait for a fortnight,
then escape to the mountains.

If I'm questioned,
I'll simply produce the paper.
Malaga? Never been there.

Then I remember.
The blood from my lips
to my toes runs ice cold.

Papa's *paper*!

Early on in my flight, I had
fastened it into my book of Hafiz
with some beeswax—
so worried was I that it might fall out.

And I have *sold* it.
I've sold it!
For less than a song.

You'll laugh at my sorrow.
The idea was desperate
anyway.

But that paper was like
a part of my skin,
once stripped from me
but, at long last, grown back.

What Price?

Some now talk of converting.
If you're baptized, they free you.
But the thought holds no temptation for me.

I've been given this option before.
In Cordoba, a friar, a young man of twenty,
lurked around near the oven
shared by our street.

He waited for slaves fetching bread for their masters.
Told us baptism was how to be free.

The Benvenistes, conversos,
weren't allowed to own Christians.
One dunk in the font—or the well, if I liked.
That's all it would take.
I'd be my own man.

Or would I?

I wanted freedom.
But not at the price of the thoughts
of my soul.

I feel the same now.
Perhaps there's still time
to go to the Queen.
Offer myself as translator.
Swear up and down I had nothing
to do with the invader's trick.

But something inside me
shrinks from this thought.
Whether I find my uncles or not:
these Malagans are my people now.

The Coming of the Inquisition (2)

There are conversos among the Malagans.
Christians who once were Jews.
They all must report, it's announced,
to the Gibralfaro.

Many conversos once fled
Castile for Malaga. They felt themselves safer
under Muslim rule.

Now monks and officials move through the crowd.
One stops, looks at me
in my Christian garb. I shake my head,
wish him *Salaam Aleikum*—
"Peace be with you" in Arabic.
He moves on.

That night, the rest of us hear how it's gone.
The conversos were put into shackles
as soon as they walked through the doors
of the fortress. Now they wait in its dungeons
for their trials to start.

Trials for what?
Charges have not yet been laid.
But the Inquisitors "know"
there is heresy here.
These conversos, they say, have lived
many years outside the reach of the Office.
Who can doubt, poor souls,
that they've erred?

The proof, so they say,
will come out in the trials.

Isn't that having the cart
pull the horse?

A date has been set
for an *auto-da-fé*—Malaga's first.
Who's to say Muslims who choose to convert
won't be on the way to the fires themselves?

All who agree to baptism

are donning the shoes of conversos.
As Christians, they're subject
to trial by the Office.

Most priests don't
or won't
speak our language.

I've had good fortune.
I speak Spanish.
But how will these others
learn all the rules
for being "good Christians"?
Good Christians enough
to stay off the stake?

Degrees of Ugliness

I thought I'd seen every
ugliness known to this land.
But some lay in wait.

There are men here who sell their wives to the soldiers
to raise enough money to ransom themselves.
That's not the worst.
A few sell their daughters.
The soldiers bargain, and do what they want,
and then throw the girls, and their clothes, back into
the yard.

Sometimes they cast a coin or two down:
much less than the price that was named.
Those who protest eat a sword in the throat
as their last meal on Earth.

The Sea?

There is talk that the Crown puts its slaves on the sea.
The armada needs strength to power its galleys.
Spain's coastline is growing with all this conquest.
It must be defended.

Some say it's a fate far worse than death.
Others are hopeful.
At least a ship is not always chained to a shore.

But these galleys do nothing but sail back and forth.
They look out for pirate ships manned by us "Moors."

I've heard that the oars of the slaves carry long,
woeful tales.

One slave scratches words into wood—just a few.
The man after him keeps on where those stopped.

Here's what I take from this bit of news:
galley slaves die in less time
than wet wood takes to rot.

A New Music

What more can we do?
We talk and we sing and we pray
and we dance—those few of us
with the strength left to stand.

Some men play a music like none I've yet heard.
Or, like all musics rolled into one.
The same language-soup I'd speak with Papa,
those long, late nights of shared study.
A dash of Arabic. A dollop of Spanish.
And a pinch of Ladino—the everyday tongue
of the Spanish Jews.

One hot afternoon, a woman with skin
the ripe brown of a raisin
sings in a voice so like the call of the muezzin
I'm shocked.

I said to Solitude:
Come live with me!
At least, that way, we'll be two.

She sits on the ground.
But her sound scrapes the floor of the heavens.

Night Voices

With the last torch extinguished
the guitar strums to life
once again.

People call out their verses
from all parts of the yard.

Since we can't see the author,
it seems we all sing.

I cried for Death
but God said
I didn't deserve her.

The sadder the words,
the more comfort they carry
on the bend of their backs.

Detained

Before I know I am singing,
I am. The words just fly out.

I called out for Death
but Death was detained.

His Highness Fernando
had made death his slave!

A sad laugh greets my words.
It warms me, somehow.

Another voice sings:

I offered to free him—
the price was too high.

There's an answer to that,
farther off. I'm asleep before
I can hear how it goes.

I Sing

Our lives in Granada were once filled with song.
Music as common as dust in the sky.
It filled up the streets and the courtyards
and even the caves carved into the hills.

Mother's voice was an arrow that pierced to the heart.
When my *abba* went missing, we sang songs together.
We had each other. Our songs were our hope: he'd
be back.

But when those men took my mother,
song died in my throat.
That was that, so I thought.

How could I sing one single note?
After they'd struck her? Pulled our heads by the hair?
Branded our cheeks, her smooth skin, with rods
dipped in fire?

My Cordoban family did not hear me sing.
If a song knocked at my heart, I would chase it.
There's no place for you here.

But the raisin-skinned woman has taught me.
Song needn't be joyful.

I think of my parents each minute I live.
I'll sing now for them.

Time Eight months!
The Queen, it is said, has bought us some time.

If we find the King's price in those months,
we go free.

If not,
we are theirs—
for all time.

Trick Our eight-month reprieve, we are told,
is not to be spent lounging round
with guitars.

But how we're meant to raise money
when we're chained to these benches
is anyone's guess.

For they've done it.
They've put us to work on the sea.

The war is still on:
the armada needs every ship
on the water.

I start to wonder.
Was the ransom no more
than a masterful ruse?
What a way to make sure
that none of the conquered would hide their wealth!

No coins or rich silks buried
in caves, like in tales of Aladdin.
The Malagans owned up to every last shred
so they might meet the sum.
The spoils of a lifetime of good fortune, fine
climate, hard work.

The Crown said it wasn't enough.
And then took it.

Wormholes

A man, the tribune, beats out time
with a gavel. We follow his raps
with our strokes.

My oar is not covered with tales.
But the first weary morning,
weak light shines through wormholes in the hull.

There, on my oar's blade—a message.
It's written in Latin,
but I can translate.

Oft was I weary when I toiled at thee.

I wonder if these nine small words
hold the sum of my fate.

Freedom Dream

What sleep we're allowed is done sitting up,
still chained to our oars.
We're not picky. We gulp down these hours
as if they were food.
At first, I don't dream.
I'm too tired for that.

But one night, I do.
It's not fair. With such
little sleep I should dream of
hot baths, or beautiful maidens
swathed in soft silk.

Instead comes Ramon.
He is gouging the earth with his fingers.
"It's down here somewhere," he says.

"It will buy you your freedom."
He scratches and claws.
I am angry. I walk off.
But his shout calls me back.
"Here it is!" He is grinning.

In his hand is the rough stone of pumice
we used, as scribes, to rub out our mistakes.

The Stone

In the morning, I'm startled.
The tribune hands me—
a large pumice stone!
Am I some kind of prophet?

My eardrum explodes.
The man has just struck me.
"Don't sit there gaping!"
He grabs back the stone.
This time he accosts
my sore ear with a shout.
"Don't understand me?
Okay. Do this, see?"
He scours the stone back and forth
on the blade of the oar.
Then gives it back, plus one last slap
for good measure.

I wish I could sharpen his head!
Better yet, pierce him with sharp words
instead.

Rhythm

Reach and then pull.
Feather the blade of the oar
and then dip.

My heart must now beat to the drum
of this rhythm.
I can't think.
I just row.

Once in a while
a song crosses my mind,
but it makes too deep a skip
in the pulse of my rowing.
I must concentrate
if I'm not to lose stride
and be wrenched with such force
that my arms may just break.

Reach and then pull.
Feather the blade of the oar
and then dip.

If the others would sing,
and keep time,
it might work.

But we're flogged if we're even
caught talking.
I've had enough lashes
for seven lifetimes.

Reach and then pull.
Feather the blade of the oar
and then dip.

When ships first plied these shores,
far back as the pharaohs,
the oarsmen were prized
above everyone else.

Well, times have changed.

Still, I must marvel
at what we men do.
Four hundred oars.
Two hundred men.
All with hearts and—
though this may be forgotten—
minds. All moving
as one.

Reach and then pull.
Feather the blade of the oar
and then dip.

Distance

I improve.
The pain arrowing
up my arms doesn't stop.
But at least now, while I row,
I can pick my own thoughts.

Or can I?
My mind seems stuck in Cordoba.
Our patio, and its small
lemon tree.

One branch of that tree
I thought of as mine.

A dove, of a brown
even lighter than dough,
came each evening.
It perched on my branch.

His cry filled my heart
with a sorrowful joy.

*How are **you?*** he would sing.
*How are **you?***

If I were that dove
I could travel back there
in three hundred raps of the gavel.
Well, more like three thousand.
But I could.

It is not all that far.
But for me, in these chains,
that lemon tree
is as far as Shiraz,
birthplace of Hafiz.
Or farther. As far as hell is
from heaven.

All the distance,
maybe, that one life can hold.

THREE

Ramon

Jerez and Malaga, Castile

1492

Dust

Jerez now.
How many cities is that?
In four years of toiling for the Holy Office
I've been moved round so much,
it feels more like forty.

The shrewd minds who maneuver
this massive machine
don't like to see us, the cogs,
stick in one place too long.

They're afraid we'll make ties.
That something will melt
our iced-over hearts.

But my nights don't belong to the Inquisition
nor to anyone else.
There's no way I'll stay put in my room.

Vast as the castles "we" take over are,
somehow the walls between
corridors and rooms
are always too thin.

So at night, I go out to escape
shouts and pleas I'd rather not hear.
I sit in bodegas, or dark, quiet taverns
off quieter plazas.

I don't wear my cloak on these outings.
I want to blend in.
I'm sick of the look people get on their faces
when they notice the badge that's sewn there.
A sword and a cross. And an olive branch—
to stand for forgiveness.
The infamous sign of the Inquisition.

People ignore me. I try to write letters
to Mama and Papa, but mostly I listen.
The talk is conversos—what else is new?

How this person said that *that* person ate this.
How that person said that *this* person ate that.
How Maria went to the rabbi's son's wedding
just ten years ago. Or was it twenty?
No difference. She'll still be condemned.

I drink wine while I sit. Don't bother, these days,
to water it down—it's not like I'm proud of the
work I do now.
I snack on *tapas* of olives and ham.
I eat pork, of late, without a third thought.
All food tastes like dust
to me now.

Work

Yes, I'm a cog.
There's no question.
But, at my desk, I have power.
That's something I once
burned to possess.

I don't like it.

They are brought to me one at a time,
as if I'm a king instead of
the lowliest scribe in the place.

Few of them weep.

But the guards yank their arms
like they'd be better off out of their sockets.

The man—or the woman—must strip, piece
by piece. I write down what comes off.

I guess I looked shocked when, one day early on,
a guard stuck his finger straight up the arse
of a prisoner. "Sometimes I find gold!" the guard
leered.
"We can't trust these Jews, now can we, señor?"

I kept my face blank as a newly made slate.
"I thought our Office dealt only with Christians," I said,
coolly as I could.

But the guard merely laughed. Made a face.
"You have only to smell, my young friend,
to know what you're dealing with here!"

Plants Remember those endless *Plants of Castile*?
Well, I thank them.

That blessed author—I forget his name now—
was so concerned with our Kingdom's tally
of lichens and ferns,
he made me a master with numbers!

I choose to believe that is why I've been given
the most boring job in the Holy Office.
It's not just because my blood is *impure*.

Other scribes talk, come nightfall.
Days, they must watch things I try not to hear.

I begin to be thankful that numbers don't lie.
The scribes claim that when torture starts,
people will say anything to make it stop.
They denounce their own mothers. Themselves.
Their children who've yet to be born.
The scribes write it down as if it were truth.

Which is just what the courts will then call it.

Language

I've heard that soon, the Office might turn
its gaze to the Moors baptized in the conquest.

Some of these New Christian Moriscos,
it's said, still pray to Allah in private.

I'm afraid. My ten or so words
of Arabic are ten more than most
of the scribes here can speak.

What if they want me for more than just lists?
I don't want to witness
any of this.

Anyway, I'm not sure
I could help.

Oftimes what I hear
from those mouths
in those rooms
doesn't sound much
like language at all.

Shame

When I saw my first *auto-da-fé*
all those years ago,
I was shocked. And aghast.
No one would argue: a man or woman
who's burning alive makes a terrible,
soul-chilling sight.

But, in my heart, I was smug.
I thought that to earn such a horrible fate,
doled out by learned men in fine robes,
a person must surely *deserve* it.

I'm so ashamed now of how blind I was.

Here is one case.
A woman of sixty.
She came in last month. I remember
she had little else than an old woolen
blanket she said was her father's.

Denounced by a neighbor, said her thin file.
Her crime?
Eating meat, one Good Friday,
when they were both girls.
That testimony was fifty years old!

Another thing: the women were known to be rivals.
They both sold their beer in the same market town.
Who's to say the denouncer
didn't want this one out of the way?

The woman was sentenced today.
She did not confess.
And so, guilty or not, she'll be burned.

Letters

I don't blame Papa
for hating me now.
He often told me:
Always be true.

And look how I'm using
the skills that he taught me.
The only art here
is the lies of the Office.

I send home letters,
and any small sums I'm able to save.
But from Papa, there's never so much
as a word in return.

Papa knows there's one thing
I need him to say.
I forgive you.
And since he can't say it,
and still be true,
he doesn't write back.

Still, I address all my letters
to both Mama and him. I won't give up.
I will find a way
to help him forgive.

Finding a Scribe

Mama, of course,
can't write me back.

She is busy, I know.
There is also the question
of finding a scribe she can trust—
and who won't charge the sky.

Papa would never consent
to write it: I know that.

For the very first time
I wish women were taught,
like us men, how to write.

There are nights when I so
long for news from my home
that I'd lop my scribe's hand
if Mama could have it, and use it,
instead.

Trust

One should always take care
of the wishes one makes.

No, I haven't awakened minus my fingers.
But a messenger knocks while I'm still abed.

There's a letter for me.
Mama has, after all, found a hand.

Don't be alarmed by how much I say
in this letter, she starts.

This scribe is a friend. I think
we can trust him.

Beside this, in the margin,
is written *YOU CAN.*

Water *Ramon,* she continues,
Papa's not well.
His sight only gets
worse with time.

And then there's the shaking
which he still denies.
Even when there is some small job,
he can't finish it.
His hand is too weak for the pen.

Thank you for the money for spectacles.
What an invention they truly must be!
Alas, we used it to pay Señor Ortiz. I'm sorry, Ramon.
He's raised our rent once again.

I shouldn't tell you—but our landlord is a New Christian too.
His "non-Jewish blood" goes back five generations,
but for him that's not long enough.
He wants Papa to forge his papers
to say that he's clean! Can you imagine
your papa doing such a thing?

Last week, Papa's hand shook,
tipping the glass bowl of water
he uses to magnify script.
The ink ran. I found him, Ramon,
weeping over his work.

My son, pray for your papa.
He might be angry at me
for telling you this,
but each night, in his prayers,
there is one for you.

Blackbird Pie

Mama's letter makes me feel
about as tall as a pine cone.

But we're feasting in honor
of something—
a battle's been won? A foe
of the Church, burned at the stake?
Who knows?

The rich food and wine
eclipse thoughts of all else.

We cut our pies—there's one
for each man—and live blackbirds fly out,
squawking like mad.

It's just like the feasts in stories
I once copied in our shop.
I remember my fluttering heart,
reading them. Not to mention
my grumbling belly.

Who'd have thought I would rise quite so far?
Even that Bea I was once so in love with
would be half-impressed. A hidalgo,
no less—I've lately been given a horse.

Speaking of ladies, aren't some
meant to grace feasts like this?
The stories all had them.
Our table hosts only grim monks and dull scribes.
Torturers too, just come from their chambers.

One of the blackbirds did not escape
when the door to outside was opened.
It sits on a rafter, seeming to wonder,
How did I get here?

I know just how it feels.

Job Offers

Only a day after I'd sold myself
to the Inquisitor,
Papa called me to his room.

He asked me to help him
with his life's work.

"There is a book I must send to Oman,
in Africa. There it will hide from the fires,
for a time," Papa said.
"But the passage is tricky.
We must make a copy, in case it is lost.

"Ramon, there is peril in this. I had wanted to keep
it from you, for your safety.
But we must take the chance. Please,
will you help?"

My heart filled with bile and it rose to my mouth.
"Do you not think I know
why you're asking me now?
It's because your precious Amir
isn't here—your first choice."

Papa smiled his sad smile and held out his hand.
"Come, son. It wasn't like that. My ancestor wrote
in Arabic.
Amir helped me to translate his papers.
Without the man's words,
how could I write his life's story?

"And, Ramon, you must know
I was fearful for you.
For your very life.
Those papers contained
many Hebrew words. To touch them
would mean great danger for you,
a converso. That is why I have kept them
from you for all of these years."

But I couldn't, or wouldn't, give in to him.
I hardened my heart.

"I can't help you," I told him,
not meeting his eyes.
"The Holy Office
is my master now."

Lost Another letter arrives.
It's left on the tray
with my hot chocolate.

I'm ashamed to admit
that I dread to read it.
I drink the chocolate
down to its dregs
before I do.

Dear Ramon,

Once I thought people got,
in the end, the life
they deserved.

It's not true.
Look at your papa.
His misfortunes pile up—-
we can't see overtop them.

We've heard from his uncle
in Africa—the one he sent
his book to, remember?
It wasn't received. It
must have been lost in the mails.

Papa worked on that book
for many long years.
Whenever we'd meet a Mudejar friend
in the street, Papa would ask
some word's definition. Our walks were quite slow.
You can imagine my gladness
when Amir came!

The book told the life of your great ancestor.
A great scribe. A friend to all peoples. A great man.
You know all that.

Your papa translated that book from
scraps of old letters
he'd hid in his room. Your ancestor
was a Jew. You know that too.

What you don't know, Ramon, is that
three months ago, the Holy Office
came into this house. They found all those letters.
They were Arabic, but with some Hebrew words.
They couldn't read them. No matter. They were burned.

Papa was spared because of his health.
But now he must wear that cursed yellow garment
—the sanbenito*—when he goes out.*

Ramon, your papa is tired of the lies
being written.
Now those presses that print
hundreds of books at one time
are becoming the norm.
Never mind what that means
for all scribes.
The worst of it is, lies can now spread
a hundred times faster!

Papa says stories of good, quiet men
don't sell books.
The public prefers the fantastic—like tales of Jews who eat babies!
A much better sell, don't you think?

Ramon, I don't know
why I'm writing all this.
I know you must work, and your job
keeps us fed.

We love you.

Mama.

Consequence

Without the help
that I wouldn't give,
there was no time for a copy.

Papa's fear of arrest
grew with each day that passed.

So he sent it.
The story of our ancestor's life.
The greatest work of Papa's own.

Now, thanks to my wounded pride,
it is gone. And my hope
that one day he'd forgive me—

lost along with it.

Moving

I've just had word—
I'm off to Malaga.
The other scribes, too,
have been told to pack up.

We'll be scattered all over, as always.
But, consulting that night, we discover
one thing our new homes-to-be
have in common.

They're all on the sea.

Heaven

The fortresses still overflow
with heretics they found
when they won back Malaga
four years ago.

Instead I am given a room
in the home of a kind Christian lady.
It is heaven!

The sole screams I can hear
belong to the seabirds outside
my window, diving in the wind.

Wandering

I wait to find out
what my job will be here.

To kill time, I comb the bookstalls
near the docks.

There's not much.
Romances long cast aside
by fickle fashion. An uncontroversial
prayer book or two.
No tomes on why conversos are devils,
I'm happy to say.

I'm just taking leave of the starved-looking man
who stands at one stall when my eye
lights on something familiar.

It looks much, much older than it did years ago,
like it has been shot from a cannon.

But that Arabic *H* on the cover—
I'd know it anywhere.

Damn my eyes. The seller has seen
them spark, I expect.
His price is five times what I'm paid
in a month. I can't meet it.

H stares in reproach,
like one rung of a ladder
I know I must climb.

The man seems to know
what's coming next. He smiles
a wide smile.

Amir, you're determined to keep me
in my humble place, I just know it.
First my knife, and now this!
No Castilian can call himself a hidalgo—
a worthy man—when he has no horse!

Poem (2)

I try to think of a question
to pose to Hafiz, but I can't
hold a thing in my mind.

I open the book near the back.
Perhaps in his answer I'll find
my own question.

My scant Arabic is creaky with rust.
Will I understand? My heart pounds.

What is this?
Is this not the book, after all?
Oh, my horse!

Wait. Lift the first pages.
Yes, it's Hafiz.
But this stuff at the back—
the letters are tiny, the ink faint and cheap.
I must squint hard to read it.

There are times
when peace just becomes
a broken mouthful.
A word that no tongue in the world
can pronounce.
A.

Cover to Cover

I read Hafiz cover to cover.
I can decipher about every third word.
Most of it would be too deep for me,
anyway, even if it were in Spanish.
Including the poems at the back!
They must be Amir's—at the foot
of each one is the simple brushstroke
of the Arabic *A*.

But one thing gets through
this thick skull.

A page is glued near the back
of the book.

Before I read even one word,
my heart flips in my chest
like it's taken a kick.

The writing I'd know anywhere.

The words are in Spanish, and
then written again, more awkwardly,
in Arabic.

I, Isidore Benveniste, hereby manumit Amir,
son of Aman Ibn Nazir of Granada.

The page is dated 1486.
Just months before
I ordered my "slave" to meet Beatriz.

He was free. Why didn't he tell me
to shove that damned knife
up my ignorant arse?

Sleepless Once More

His bright, burning cheekbone under my hand.
Over and over—the feel and the sound.
As if I am the one being hit.

The mark of the slave on his face.
Right under my blow.

The feel of his face and
the sound of my hand.

The look on his face.

The slammed, silent door
of his back. Straight, and proud,
and leaving
forever.

Cross For four years I have tried
to banish that day
from my mind.

When Amir failed to come home,
I was fuming. My Toledo knife!
But I wasn't surprised.

He'd always been proud.
And I'd struck him!
He'd run away.
Or so I thought.

I saw Bea in passing,
a couple days later.
She saw me too.
Crossed the street to avoid me.

That did it.
I guessed Amir had run off
without giving my present.
So she was angry.

I was shocked to discover
that I didn't care.
I'd already started
my work at the Office.

My romance with Bea
seemed like something
from childhood, a
memory of too much rich candy
on a feast day.

Siesta

When I began my work
with the Office,
I continued to live
with Papa and Mama.
But I felt like an exile
in my own home.

Papa stayed in his room.
Did not talk to me.

I knew that they hated this job,
and blamed me, as well, for Amir's
leaving us.

They didn't know
I had struck him.
But I knew that they knew
it was some deed of mine
that made him go.

During siesta, I haunted the streets.
I was walking one day, in no hurry,
when Bea saw me.
This time she didn't walk past.
In fact, she rushed up behind me.
I kept walking.

"Ramon, stay.
Don't you know how sorry I am?"

She shocked me with what she said next.
There were some men, and when
she gave Amir—a Moor, after all—
her white handkerchief, they must have
assumed—

"Where is he?"

"You don't know? But I thought—"

"He's been gone since that night, Bea.
I can't believe you've not told me—
he might have been killed!"

"Oh, no! It's all right! I saw him get up, walk away.
You know—after."

"You *saw* him? You mean,
you stood there and watched?"

"Ramon, keep it down. People will hear you.
I was afraid. I hid. What are you getting
so angry about? *I* didn't beat him! For heaven's sake!

He's only a Moor!"

I'd heard enough.
"He's my friend, Bea, okay?
My *friend*."
She looked confused.
"But I thought—"

"Never mind what you thought.
I wish you health.
Good-bye and good luck."

I stormed off.
Well, sort of.

"Ramon!"

I was weak. I turned round.

"If he ever returns—"
"Yes?"

"Can I have back my tooth?"

Arrest Her *tooth*?
I didn't ask.

And that was the last time I saw her.

But I did see her father, months after that,
not long before leaving Cordoba.

That fine *familiari*
was being led into prison
by two guards with swords.

I got a glimpse
of the cell where they put him.
Later that day, I detoured
so I'd pass it.

Someone within—it could have been him—
was sobbing like a child.

Small Stories

Each day, I report to the Office.

twelve silver bracelets
a small rusted chain
one silver dagger
sixteen pewter spoons

One lady shivers through a flimsy cloak
that makes an *old sack* look like a fur coat.
Between her and me, a delicate brooch.
It looks like a beetle
crouched there on the desk.

The lady says,
Write it all down, please,
just as I tell you.

A brooch, yellow-gold backing, in the form of a tree,
comprising eleven small corals,
received from Señora Alvaro de Mansares, a Christian seamstress,
on the occasion of the owner's—former owner's—
wedding to Jusef de Ormada, a Jew, now in
exile in Portugal with their daughters, aged fourteen and twelve.

If only I had more paper, I could write down
these people's whole lives.
(Though this lady's entry comes close.)

Papa would like that, I think:
small stories instead of tall tales.

Hope Before curfew, I'm down at the docks.
Finding Hafiz was a sign.
Amir *must* have been here.
I'll find him too.

I've been asking questions.
Most of the Moors who lived or passed through here
were taken as slaves for the ships.

My heart says there is hope.
Hafiz, is there hope?

Let's not let Reason deter us:
That judge has no jurisdiction here.

That strains my brain quite a bit.
But I think it means *Yes, there is.*

Sewing

I scare up a needle and thread—
two more weapons I've no clue how to use.

I'm determined to mend this Hafiz.
I've pictured the moment so many times.
Me finding Amir. And rescuing him.
And then, like the icing on top of a cake,
producing Hafiz! But the book
falling apart in my hands—or his—
is not part of the play.

Señora Brabiste, the lady I lodge with,
sees me fighting to shove the fine point of the needle
through the leather cover.
It suddenly seems as tough as a brick.
She takes pity.

"Here, let me," she says gently.
Her fingers are nimble; she seems to grow younger
each moment she works.

But soon she is frowning.
"The pages are strong," she says,
"but this cover has been through too much.
I'll stitch it for now, but soon you will need
to replace it."

Familiar

The ships' captains begin
to know me by sight.

They scowl when I near them.
"Go away!" they admonish.
"How many times have I told you?
There's no one here who fits that description."

I have told them my name is Señor Ortiz,
that I search for a slave who is rightfully mine.
(I wear the Office's cloak inside-out on these trips.)
He was stolen, I've said, by bandits.
And I need this particular one for my work.
Has anyone seen him? There's an *S* on his cheek—
his left, I believe. And he speaks
both Spanish and Arabic.

I don't go so far as to tell them he writes.
Best not to plump up his worth
in their greedy minds.

Trick of the Light

There is talk that the Office
is looking more closely at books.

Jewish content is no longer all
that marks them for the List.

There is Protestantism, Messianism, Occultism,
and altogether more isms that I ever thought
walked this whole world.

It's clear time's run out for Hafiz.
He's Muslim, yes, but it's more than that.
Some people think using a book
to divine the future—even just for a game—
is devil's play.

An idea hovers in the back
of my mind.

Two nights ago,
I dreamt of that book of Papa's:
the life of my ancestor.
Because of me, lost.

In the dream, though,
there Papa's book was.

Floating between
the lines on the page

like a trick of the light
when I opened Hafiz.

Sewing (2)

Then, yesterday, I chanced
to look up from my writing.

The prisoner there was tucking some treasure
into the hem of his tunic.

He blanched when he saw
that I saw. Our eyes met.

I said nothing.
But it planted a seed
in my head.

Calm

I am looking for something to calm me,
I tell her.

Well, there are herbs—

No, I mean something to do with my hands,
in the evenings. Besides writing, I add.

She looks at my fingers,
all stained with ink, and she nods.

I go on.
Pardon me for my rudeness, but something struck me
that day, when you mended my book.
The peace on your face has stayed with me.

Señora, do you think
I could learn how to sew?

Space

Paper is scarce—that hasn't changed.
The Office tracks each sheet
they give us.

But the poems of Hafiz
are quite short.

Each page of his book
holds more empty space
than inked words!

Like a doctor unstitching a wound,
I unsew him.

These spaces are what I will use
to record at least part
of my prisoners' lives.

Small Stories (2)

I ask them to tell me the story
of one of the things that I'm taking away.

I hear stories of courage and stories of love,
tales of betrayal and greed, and of death.
Sometimes of people just getting along.

Stories of parents, who thought everything
would be different by now.
Of children, who they hope
can survive this somehow.

All to do with one simple thing
they once owned.

One woman was dragged from her bed
and baptized in the faded silk slippers
she's just handed over.

All through these sessions,
the guard at the door merely snores.
I know that this man
has a fondness for ale.

Well, Papa, it turns out strong drink
is the friend of this scribe, after all!

I write in the tiniest hand I can manage.
I hope to cram dozens of these
onto one single page.

Every night, in my room, I tear off
the portion I filled in that day.

Then unstitch the hem
of my Unholy cloak.

Into its lining
their stories go.

Water Rat

Here he comes, they exclaim.
Señor Water Rat, at it again!

In these last few weeks
I've near given up hope.
And I must say—
the jeers of the crews
grate upon me.

But a new galley ship
has pulled into port.
Of course, I must check,
though my heart is not in it.

Hafiz, have you led me
so far astray?

Wolf This captain strikes me as more
wolf than man.

When I give the description
for the hundredth time,
he eyes me with interest.
I can't say I like it.
I'm not that surprised when he says,
"Follow me."

It isn't the first time I've been in a galley.
One or two captains before him—
much nicer men—have led me below
to search as I pleased.

But each time, it shocks me.
This ship is worse than the others.
The slaves, as is custom,
are shackled with chains to the benches
they sit on.
There aren't seats for all.
Some of them stand in their irons.
They're given no choice
but to sleep on their feet.

The stench is amazing.
Hundreds of men, crammed in this place
for months upon end.
No baths for them, you can bet.

But the very worst thing is the look in their eyes.
Or, should I say, the absence of a look.
Here are men who are worked
till they're no longer men.

Or, so I think.
One has just kicked me—very hard—
in the shin!
I look at their faces, expecting a glimmer
of something in one.
But they're all back to blank, blank,
blank.

"You going to survive?" laughs the captain.
"Well, here he is.
This is your man, I expect."
He points to a decrepit old twig
who looks to be two sleeps from death.
"Been roughed up a bit.
I'll let you have him again for less than the price
of a horse."

I'm walking away in a huff when it happens.
Have you ever played Egg?
I once did, with Bea.
One person—it always works better
if it is a girl—pretends that she's cracking
an egg on your head. Then she shivers
her fingers all over your back.
You'd swear it was egg yolk trailing down your skin.

That's exactly the feeling I get
in the moment before
I turn and lock eyes
with Amir.

No Sale

Of course I've no papers
to prove that he's mine.

(Though I do have a paper
—I don't say this—
to prove that he's not.)

This wolf wants an arm and a leg for Amir.
I couldn't meet it if I saved
all my pay for a year.

All through this horrible haggling
I feel Amir's eyes on the back of my head.
I can just hear his thoughts:
Good old Ramon, now trading in slaves
instead of just trying to boss them around!

Desperate

I take Hafiz back to the stall
where I bought him.

When the bookseller sees
the pages I've torn
for my secret stories,
he laughs in my face.

"What have you used
this poor treasure for?
Archery practice?"

I offer to take
only half what I paid.
"I'm desperate," I plead.

"Who isn't these days? Look, my friend.
The truth is, as soon as you bought this,
I sold your fine horse.
And so made more money that day
than I did all year. Okay?
No one buys books anymore.
Least of all ones in the Arabic tongue.
Now—God and Allah be with you.
Please get lost."

Ink

I don't cease my work with the stories,
but I have to admit that my heart's not quite in it.

The cramped little letters seem to crawl through
my fingers, then sink in sharp claws.
By the end of the day I can barely lift up the needle
to sew them away.

I ask Saint Katarina for help.
She's the patron of scribes,
though I've always thought her a curious choice.

When the Byzantine Emperor cut off her head,
her blood gushed out white as cow's milk.

I think if you cut off *my* head
a river of ink would pour out.

There's so much left on my fingers by nightfall,
my bedsheets are spotted with black when I wake.
Starry sky in reverse.

Still, I pray.
To her, and to anyone up there who'll
listen.
What more, in this life, can I do?

Tremble

At the end of one workday
I look at the piles of fine objects before me.
Then I look at the guard. Sleeping, as always.
It's normally me
who must rouse him.

There's a necklace—
taken from one Señora Aldez.

The story she told
was rather dull.

But the treasure itself—

It sits
whispering.

It could—
I am certain—
buy back Amir.

My hand trembles:
not just from my work
with the words.

I take it.

Temper Maybe wives' tales about wolves
have some truth. They say they smell fear.

As soon as the captain
sees me on the dock, he starts to roar.

Get the hell out of here!
I'm in no mood for you.

But—

No buts!
If I set foot
on his ship one more time—
even in *front* of his ship—
he will kill me.

I believe him.

I'm so shaken up
I do a dense thing.

I throw the necklace
into the sea.

I've already turned in
the ledger today.
Someone, not long from now,
will read it and ask what's become
of the treasure of Señora Aldez.

Proclamation

We are permitted to leave our posts
for the herald's announcement.

One monk is verily hopping with glee.
"Get out there, my boys! It's not
every day you can witness
the making of history!"

I've grown accustomed
to shrinking stories
into a few lines.

I'll do the same here.

By July 31—that's six months from now—
every Jew left in Spain must be gone from her shores.

It is rumored that Don Abravanel, the wealthiest Jew
remaining in Spain, had very near changed
the mind of the Queen.

If she let the Jews stay, the Don promised,
he would raise enough money to pay for five wars.
Every maravedi would go to the Crown.

At that moment, the Inquisitor Torquemada
rushed into the room. Threw three pieces of silver
at the Queen's feet. "So, too," he hissed,
"Judas sold Christ for a few coins."

Torquemada knows well the heart of the Queen.
His little drama worked like the charm
of a wizard.
"Our mind is made up," she was heard to intone.
"In six months' time, all Jews must go."

A Thought

So many ships are crammed in the port
I nearly lose track of which one's Amir's.

Jews pour into Malaga from all over Spain.
They make right away for the ships.
Places are scarce; their chance for a square of ship floor
is too easy to miss.

And the journey is much worse by land.
Bandits hide there; they'll slit your belly.
Everyone knows, goes the thinking,
that Jews swallow gold!

It burns me to think of the greedy wolf-captain
reaping reward from this misery.
His ship, like them all,
is near full up already.

Here's a thought.
What if I posed as a Jew, unbaptized,
waiting to flee like the rest?
It would at least get me onto that ship
with Amir!

Sewing (3)

It's back to the Cordoban days,
when I spent all my nights caged indoors,
holed up like a girl.

My last night on dry land, if all goes well.
How do I spend it?
Not drinking, or fighting, or
chasing women.
I'm *sewing*!
I wonder what some of the tough torturers
I feast with would say to that!

My words frame Hafiz's like
arabesques you see in the fanciest books.
I've used only half of the pages so far,
but I'm praying that Papa will think them
a start.

Perhaps I should mail them to him
before my next move.
But remember what happened to *his*
precious book. Better not.

One last time, I open the hem of my cloak.
In go these stories. Plus Amir's poems,
and Papa's letter making him free.

I am ready.

Inspector I storm on the ship
like my time is pure gold.
"Make way, people, please.
Make way!"
A friar is tailing the Jews as they walk
up the plank. One last chance at conversion!
Him, too, I push past.

Of course, it hasn't been
quite as hasty as this.
I've been hiding, watching the ship,
since the dawn.
I know that captains on duty
keep logs of events even when they're ashore.
They write in these books three or four times
each day.

So I waited until the wolf
had descended below.
Then seized my chance.
And it's worked!
I am on.

I didn't prepare
for what might come next.
A hundred Jews cram here
in the hold. There's scarcely
enough air to share for a day.

Now all of their eyes are aimed at me,
and, more sharply, the crest on my cloak.
I see fear, and hatred,
and the end of hope.
Someone spits.

With their eyes still upon me
I take off the cloak.
Turn it inside out.
Hope no one remarks
on the patchwork of thread at the hem.

Still they scowl. I want to shout.
Believe me, I'd like nothing more
than to volley this trophy of the Office
straight into the sea.

But I can't.
Inside this one hateful garment
lie the scraps of my hope.
They are all that I have
to win back the love of my father.

Jerusalem!

I crouch in a corner
of the ship's hold.
If I go long enough without moving,
I reason, these Jews will forget me.

They do.
They gather instead
around a young couple.
Four men hold an old,
tattered quilt by its corners
to shelter their heads.
I have heard Jews are wed
beneath canopies.
Could this makeshift event
be that holy rite?

There's a smiling old man
in the center of things. Now
a small glass is placed at his feet.
He stomps and it shatters.
Everyone shouts, *Jerusalem!*
There is singing and dancing
well into the night.

These people are joyful
because they are one.
They may no longer have houses,
or even a country.

But their customs—right down
to each shard of that glass—
are their own.
Is there not, in those,
a kind of home?

I don't know these customs.
I don't belong here.
But then,
where do I?

Missing

Only one touch is missing
from this wedding—
something to eat!

Four more months until July 31.
What will we live on? Good cheer?
Shattered glass?

Friend I see the next morning how we'll survive.
A crate with stale bread and a barrel of water
are left in the doorway, as if we are pigs.

I don't want to stand out
until I form a plan.
I stay put.
Who needs to eat *every* day?

The hold's twice as hot
as an armpit in hell.
I can't help it. I drowse.

When I wake, at my side
there's a chunk of stale bread.

A young boy smiles to himself
as I eat.
I don't merit his kindness.
Oh, well.

The stomach, I learned
long ago,
has no soul.

Move

I've been here for six days
and not made a move.
I must come up with a plan—any plan—
soon!

And what of these Jews?
No one knows when this ship will set sail.
Who's to say we won't sit here in this hold
the four full months more?

These people won't make it.
The weather gets warmer.
They start to fall ill.

One night I'm so hot I'm sure I will burst
like a blister. Has the fever bit me?

I smell smoke. I bolt up. I'm awake.

The ship is alight.
Someone screams.

"Fire!" goes the call.
Everywhere, panic. Women
and men charge like animals
for the single door to the deck.
Far above, I hear splashes of some who've got out,
throwing themselves in the sea.

Can't they go faster?
Just behind me, part of the hold's roof collapses.
A beam licks the air with a fiery tongue.

I'm almost through. Then I remember—
the slaves. Who will unchain them?

Keys

At last I'm on deck.
It's just like a scene
from a painting. Not a nice one.
A scene of the end of the world.

My eyes scour the crowd for the bosun.
I've been haunting ships long enough
—one man, I know, keeps the keys.

The wolf-captain sees me.
He screams in outrage, pointing my way.
This man is mad! Who cares that I'm here
in the midst of all this?

I was wrong. The keys to this ship
aren't kept by the bosun.
The wolf lifts a great ring of them
over his head. He looks straight at me.

And he pulls back his thick, tree-trunk arm.
Throws the keys, far as he can, into
the sea.

Last Masterpiece

A scream rends the air.

A child lies in flames
at my feet.

I recognize him.
It's the boy who left bread
by my side in the hold.

Even were he the captain himself—
or the Inquisitor Torquemada—
I know what Papa
would want me to do.

One quick look around me
I see only slaves.
I have no time to wonder
how they got free. What concerns me
is what they wear. Nothing
but raggedy cloth at his loins, every one.

So I've no choice.
Unclasp the pin at my throat.
Take a deep breath.
Then lunge on the boy.
I smother the flames
with my last masterpiece.

My fine cloak
and its contents:
ashes and smoke.

Death's Boat

I watch the boy rise.
Without a look back
he jumps into the water.

Flecks of burnt cloth trail behind
like a faithful flutter of the tiniest bats.

He swims toward something:
I can't quite make it out.
By the light from the fire
I see a black shape.

Is it a boat?
If it is, who mans it?
Is it the vessel I've read of so often
in stories—the one that is steered
by Charon, Death's servant?
It takes you across the Sea of Forgetting—
straight to hell.

Well, what hell could be worse
than this burning ship?
Flames hug the heels
of my boots.

I, too, jump in and swim.

Reach

The sea churns with wild limbs.
All still alive make for the shadow boat.

Though my boots weigh me down,
somehow I manage.
I stay afloat.

I can see, now, a hand.
It performs the same motion
again and again.
The hand is held out.
A desperate arm grasps it.
The swimmer is pulled
up to the life raft.

It's my turn.
The hand reaches.
The man it belongs to
is looking behind him.
"Squeeze in. Make room.
Lie upon one another
if you have to."

It takes me a moment to grasp
what he's said:
the words are Arabic.

I hesitate.
When the man feels
that his hand is still empty,
he looks.
And so once again
I am facing Amir.

Both of us wait—for a heartbeat.
Men more deserving
clamor for help just behind me.

I will drop my arm and turn back.
I decide that.

But Amir grabs it first
with two hands
and I'm up.

Moment Jews, a few crewmen, and
many slaves.
We squat on this raft thick as fish
in a net.

Far more were trapped on that ship.
It burns on the shore, their funeral pyre.

Most of our raftmates watch it with wide eyes,
unable not to.
But Amir and I, though our faces are turned to the ship,
watch each other.

I finally ask. "How did you do it?"
He holds out his palm.
An old friend is there:
a pumice stone.
But it's chiseled into
a very fine point.
Fine enough, I don't doubt,
for picking padlocks.

"We've been unlocked for days,"
Amir says. "Awaiting our moment.
Then the moment chose us."

Divining (2)

Behind on the shore
waits the life of Ramon,
still scribe of the Office.
Warm beds. Singing pies.
Maybe, one day, a girl
with blonde hair to sit by the fire
and sew.

Ahead, not a thing
but the sea.
Its face dark and blank.
It gives no sign to guide me.

So I look, once again, at Amir.
He looks back, closely,
as if he's divining
the book of Hafiz.

I have no answers for him.
Nor he for me.
But this very blankness—
is it not a new page
upon which to begin?

Epilogue

THREE EVENTS OF HISTORIC IMPORTANCE took place in Spain in one year, 1492. Granada, the last stronghold of the Muslims in Europe, was conquered by the armies of Queen Isabella and King Fernando: all of Spain was now Christian. Months later, Spain's remaining Jews were expelled from all of her kingdoms. And explorer Christopher Columbus, backed by Isabella and said to have been financed, in part, by conversos, set sail to discover a passage to China over the Ocean Sea.

Countless Jews lost their lives in the aftermath of the expulsion. Some of the boats they were crammed into did indeed burn before they'd even left shore; others were set on fire deliberately while at sea. Jews, including women and children, were robbed, beaten, and killed by pirates at sea and by bandits on land. And while some did receive hospice in places throughout the Muslim Ottoman Empire, others were chased away from the shores and towns where they landed. Many Jews settled in Portugal, where at first they were welcomed. But King Manuel ordered the forced conversion of all Jews in that country only five years later, in 1497.

In the 1500s, the Inquisition turned its attention to Spain's remaining Muslims. There were towering bonfires of Muslim books, as there had been of Jewish books a century before. A sweeping campaign of forced conversions was undertaken throughout the country, and by 1526 the Muslim religion had officially ceased to exist in Spain. The Moriscos, as the Christianized Muslims were now called, became the next focus of the Inquisition, and many thousands were tried and sentenced. But even this failed to satisfy Spain's quest for Christian purity. In 1609, the expulsion of all remaining Moriscos in Spain was decreed.

Ironically, Spain's Golden Age did not survive these expulsions. Many historians speculate that it took centuries for Spain to recover from the great loss of skill, strength, and knowledge that went along with the expulsion of the Muslims and the Jews (not to mention the murders of so many conversos).

The Holy Office of the Spanish Inquisition was not fully abolished until 1834, making it the longest-enduring Inquisition in history. Through the more than 350 years of its existence, it took the lives and livelihoods of hundreds of thousands of Spanish subjects.

Like the clerks of Nazi Germany, the archivists of the Inquisition kept voluminous records. But how can we trust, ask historians, confessions that were exacted under torture, or under fear of terrible repercussions if the all-powerful Inquisitors did not hear what they wanted to hear?

To walk today through the winding, history-soaked streets of Cordoba—indeed, of any Spanish city—is to witness the truth of Spain's mixed cultural heritage. It lives on today in the faces of its citizens, in its food, art, music, and architecture. All of these bear the fascinating influences of the Muslim and Jewish peoples and remind us of the time before "the Spain of three cultures" was lost.

ACKNOWLEDGMENTS

For valued assistance during the writing of this book, I wish to thank the following organizations and people: the Canada Council for the Arts, the Ontario Arts Council's Writers' Reserve program, the Markin-Flanagan Distinguished Writers Program at the University of Calgary, the Banff Centre for the Arts, the City of Ottawa, the Ottawa International Writers Festival, Dean Cooke, Roberta Major, Doug Little and Louise Thibault-Little, Susan and Edward Norman, Lise Rochefort and Adrian Jones, Dianne Bos and Harry Vandervlist, and, at every step, Peter Norman. And the deeply generous Stephen Brockwell, who sent me to Spain.

Special thanks for vision, talent, and faith to everyone who made this book a reality, especially Barbara Pulling, Heather Sangster, Shelagh Armstrong, and the entire truly remarkable team at Annick.

Hundreds of excellent books and articles were consulted in the researching of this book, but the two books I returned to again and again for both inspiration and direction were *The Origins of the Inquisition in Fifteenth-Century Spain* by Benzion Netanyahu and *The End of Days* by Erna Paris.

My research would not have been possible without the Ottawa and Calgary public libraries and the university libraries of Ottawa, Carleton, and Calgary.

Please support libraries!

About the Author

Melanie Little has been hailed as an author who might "very well become the Alice Munro of our generation." She has won numerous awards for her essays and short fiction. Her essays for young adults have appeared in two anthologies by Annick Press, *Certain Things About My Mother* and *Nerves Out Loud*, which received the Book of the Year Award from *ForeWord* magazine and was included in The New York Public Library's Books for the Teen Age list.

Her highly acclaimed short-story collection, *Confidence*, was named a *Globe and Mail* Best Book and was shortlisted for the Danuta Gleed Award. In 2005–6, she was the Markin-Flanagan Canadian Writer-in-Residence at the University of Calgary. She continues to work with other writers through workshops, classes, and consultations. This is her first book for young adults.

Little currently lives in Calgary.